Among the Zinnias

Linda Fagioli-Katsiotas

The characters and events portrayed in this book are fictitious.
Any similarity to real persons, living or deceased, is coincidental
and not intended by the author.

ISBN 10: 0989219445
ISBN 13: 978-0989219440
Cover art by https://pixabay.com/en/zinnias-bunch-flowers-blooming-616470

Thank you Nick,
for your never ending love,
encouragement and support.

CHAPTER 1

Giovanna Boeri wanted to turn and leave the harbor but her feet would not allow her to do so. They were planted firmly on the wooden boards as she stood on the pier with her dearest friend, Maria, both of them squinting at the horizon, barely making out the small black speck of a departing ferry. And as it finally disappeared over the thin gray line between heaven and earth, Giovanna brought both hands to her chest where a twinge of discomfort grew to an intolerable ache. She glanced sideways at Maria, looking for relief. This woman had always been there, unwavering and stoic, always at her side — friends closer than sisters — as they spent most of their eighty-five years waiting.

And waiting.

For events beyond their control and few with resolution. But they waited anyway, together.

Maria was there with Giovanna, on that exact pier, close to sixty years prior, as they awaited the men's return to the island after Italy left the war. And later, when Giovanna's husband came down from the goat pasture pale and solemn, Maria was there to comfort her as they waited and never received an explanation for his bloody hands and clothing smeared with bits of bone and flesh.

And in these more recent years, Maria had been at Giovanna's side to walk the village path to the church, every day lighting candles and whispering novenas, kneeling against the back of the dark wooden pew, waiting for God to cure the ailing brain of Giovanna's husband.

And now Maria was at her side once again as they stood on the pier and accepted another fate that could not be changed—another long and painful wait. But this time the wait was for Angelina, Giovanna's only child, for her return to the island as she'd promised moments ago before embarking on yet another trip to America.

Giovanna sighed heavily and thought, *"Where is this place, New Jersey, and why is it so difficult for her to leave it and come home to stay?"*

Maria felt her dear friend falter as the sigh escaped into the sounds of the quiet harbor. She wrapped one arm around Giovanna's shoulder.

"She'll be back for good soon. I'm sure of it."

But that's what Maria had said months before, after Angelina's last *visit*.

*   *   *   *

Angelina stood aboard the ferry holding the railing and watching the small island grow smaller. Her mother's figure had already mixed with Maria's to become part of the gray receding rocks of the harbor. But her mother's anguish remained at her side, a permanent traveling companion.

Angelina breathed a heavy dose of sea air. What could she do? How could she help? The obligation was dead weight upon her shoulders. Her mother needed her. She knew that. But so did her children, Rocco and Patrice. She was being pulled between continents, ripped in half, unable to be whole in either.

CHAPTER 2

The blue sedan rolled toward the red traffic light as if it were steering itself. Gina held the wheel and stared up at the light, willing it to change. She was known by many in Robin's Nest, as *Plain Jane*. And yet she really wasn't—not at all. But it was a label that had been given to her, handed down in childhood, something that followed her to adulthood. And it would remain for as long as she chose to live in its birthplace.

Though some might assume, living in a place and *choosing* to live there were not at all the same. Rather, they were two different sides of a coin. But Gina knew no matter how many sides there were, it was still the same coin, and a small one at that. So there she remained.

In Robin's Nest, New Jersey.

Gina Ziti.

Her surname was from a difficult-to-pronounce, multisyllabic jumble of consonants and vowels. It had been cut to size by a well meaning immigration officer many generations before. Thus severing her heritage like a slab of meat from its bone. But with a name like Ziti, the peers of her youth could have been more imaginative when handing out nicknames.

Why *Plain Jane* then?

Gina disliked it immensely but had given up on trying to

change it or to erase the perception that was tethered to it. She was like the rural town she lived in. Its New Jersey location, to those who'd never travelled the length of the state, meant a landscape of colorless smokestacks and incinerators beneath a dirty-gray sky. Yet the tiny hamlet of Robin's Nest actually lay within a southern bed of charcoal-trunked pines. And it was more of a rolling-hills type of place with a very uncommon beauty — like Gina.

Now as she sat at the only traffic light in town, she waited patiently for it to turn green. It eventually did and Gina put her foot on the gas pedal, rolling toward Nino's Pizzeria and turning into the parking lot. She parked her car in an empty space and turned it off, glancing in the rearview mirror as she plucked the skin on her cheeks, bringing a bit of color to the surface.

Gina had tried for many years not to be *Plain Jane*. She'd attempted to change whatever body feature could be changed with her limited funds and limited courage. Lately, though, she'd grown tired of her ruby-red hair and maybe a bit too old for it. But mostly it was for that *other reason* that she'd tried to get her original color back. She'd splurged on the eighty-five-dollar beauty parlor visit last week, hoping to return her hair to its original state, of course without those random strands of gray, so maybe not exactly the original color, but close to it. The hair dye before that, the one from the minimart next to the gas station, had changed the bright red to a dirty maroon and had left the bathroom sink with splotches of brown that a good scrubbing seemed not to remedy. Even now, several days later, her husband, Joe, was still complaining about it. Well, not so much complaining as *mentioning*.

Gina left the car and walked toward the pizzeria pretending not to see Rocco behind the counter as she approached the door.

Rocco was the *other reason* — the red hair, the lip piercing, and the heavy black eyeliner — all of them gone, one at a time. He didn't like any of it. Nor did Joe. But Rocco had told her — those colors and *things covering such a lovely face,* as he put it, *no good.* Rocco had an abrupt way of saying what he liked or disliked or wanted. It was mostly because he didn't quite have the nuances of the English language, but through the listener's ear, it gave him an air of authority and decisiveness—neither of which he actually had.

From a respectable distance, he subtly peeled away Gina's layers like the scales of an onion. But an onion after all is just one layer after another. It's not like an apple where the core is rife with fiber and seeds. When the layers of an onion are gone, the onion itself is gone. But Rocco kept peeling away—a bit fascinated by the influence he had over her, not quite understanding it.

He wasn't a particularly handsome man and he knew that. He had a bit of a paunch in front of him where his belly hung over his apron strings that he tied tightly above his belt buckle. His nose was a bit big for his face and his receding black curls were salted with a few white hairs. But for Gina, he was everything Joe was not: outgoing, talkative, self-assured. Or so it appeared. Through his thick accent when he spoke to Gina over the pizzeria counter with his arms extending the warm pizza box, he seemed to have an air of belonging, though he'd only just shown up there, a few months before.

Gina wasn't even that crazy about pizza but she found herself ordering it a few times a week just to hear his voice, to hear it directed at her and to feel that warmth that seemed to emanate from the walls of the store whenever she stood at the counter.

The first time she'd seen Rocco, was a few weeks ago, two or three, she wasn't sure. He might have been there before but it wasn't until that muggy April afternoon that she'd noticed him. As she approached the store, she'd suddenly seen him looking at her and through the dark lenses on her sunglasses she watched him—watching her—from the other side of the window. He said something to the young woman next to him—his sister, Patrice. Patrice was pulling and pushing the long wooden handle of a spatula as she rearranged items in the pizza oven and she briefly looked at Gina and then at Rocco. Gina knew Patrice from the few occasions she'd been to that pizzeria but that was the first time she'd ever noticed Rocco so his enthusiastic greeting was especially baffling that day, but also very nice.

"Hello there, girl," Rocco's voice had washed over her as she walked in the door, holding it open for the person leaving. There was something familiar about him. His voice brought with it a soothing effect.

"*Girl?*" It was probably an Italian translation for something else. She hadn't been a girl for quite a while and at thirty-five, she certainly wouldn't be mistaken for a *girl* now. But she liked the sound of it — especially from him.

So that had became his usual greeting for her and that was what he said to her now as she walked through the open door — her second time that week.

"Hello, girl. We're ready for you."

"Thanks, Rocco." Gina's smile moved into her eyes.

Patrice swiped Gina's debit card and handed it back to her.

"When're you going out with me?" Rocco laughed and he placed the pizza box in her hands. He had no second line. If she'd been more forward and given him a date and time, he wouldn't have known how to proceed. He enjoyed the sense of control but didn't quite know what else to do with it.

But Gina had no answer. She said nothing as her face reddened and the warmth flowed from the hot pizza box into her arms. It was his voice, his accent, the light in his eyes when he looked at her — those were what she longed for — nothing more.

"Leave her alone." Patrice smacked the side of her brother's head with a warm towel. She'd noticed how Gina was suddenly showing up there a few times a week.

"How you doin', *Jane?*" she said.

Yes, that's right — Patrice, a young woman, much younger than Gina, more of a girl for sure, an immigrant and somewhat newcomer to Robin's Nest, someone from whom Gina ordered a pizza several times in the same week, did not know that *Plain Jane* was a nickname — an unwelcome one.

It started when Gina had ordered the first pizza from her a few months after the pizzeria had changed hands. The green and white flags stretching across the parking lot from the electric pole to the front door had attracted her attention as she drove past on her way to work. Later that day when she told Patrice over the telephone her name, Patrice thought she'd heard Gina correctly but realized her mistake when she heard two customers talking. So Gina walked into the store, just after the exchange Patrice had overheard. One woman pointing at Gina as she approached the large glass window-front had said to the other: "Isn't that *Plain Jane?*" And the other nodded in agreement.

Patrice considered herself a savvy eighteen-year-old, a modern businesswoman — not at all like the villagers back home on the island — for having remembered her language lessons and having picked up on the customers' conversation. And of course she'd already been in Robin's Nest, a very American town, for two whole months. So she wanted to show off her American English by making that new patron feel especially welcome.

As Gina walked through the door, Patrice, with a smile that went from ear to ear, took her time to clearly annunciate through her accent, "Hello, *Plain Jane*," emphasizing it all in a singsong melody, dragging it out and not at all picking up on Gina's scowl, a look that had a giant question mark behind it.

The two patrons made their way past Gina, nodding a silent greeting while trying to hide the horror on their faces. Surely Gina would know it had been from them that the pizza girl had gotten her nickname. But what else could they do? They simply did not remember her real name.

"*Really? You too?*" Gina thought as she looked at Patrice and her big welcoming eyes.

Gina's usual out-and-about public smile drew tightly into a

straight line. *"We don't even know each other."*

But Gina just paid and picked up the pizza. And if there had been another pizzeria in town she surely would not have returned to that one. In fact, she swore off pizza forever, which turned into a few days because she hadn't had any food in the house when her parents stopped by to watch the coverage of the prison break on television. It was a Saturday after all, her double shift at the hospital had just ended and take-out food was the only logical solution, though she remained steadfast in her conviction regarding pizza, which lasted until she got to the door of Happy Family Chinese Restaurant. The *closed-for-renovations* sign posted under the health department's warning brought Gina once again back to the pizzeria and that's when she first noticed Rocco.

So now Gina stood at the counter, a pizza box in her hand, back again for another whole pie, the second one that week. She really should have ordered individual slices instead. It was becoming an expensive habit. Her feet were planted on the floor and her eyes embedded in Rocco's chest. She didn't want to leave. She turned slowly and was headed toward the door when an idea popped into her head.

"Oh," she said turning back to Rocco. "You put pepperoni on it, right?" And she thought, *"just a few more minutes. That's all I want."* Why did these people have to be so efficient?

"You didn't ask for pepperoni." Patrice said. "I took the order, *Jane*. You didn't ask."

Gina turned and put the box down on the counter. "I didn't? Are you sure?"

"You never get pepperoni, *Jane*. What're you saying? This is new — the other times. You don't —"

Rocco interrupted. "You want pepperoni. You got it. Come over here. Sit down there. I'll make it nice." He pointed to a table close by and added to his sister, "She's going to get what she wants."

He winked at Gina.

At the back of the small store, an older man carrying a plastic tub pushed through a door and came toward them. The round purple edges of several onions were just visible above the lip of the container. The door led into a small kitchen. The tiny window at the top of the door was all that allowed the customers to see inside where metal shelves lined the wall. The sound that emerged from the closing door was that of water splashing—possibly a dishwasher, or a running faucet. It was part of the background noise mixing with a singer's voice that came from two small speakers perched on a table. The older man looked from Gina to Rocco and then said something to Patrice. Patrice answered him in a rapid-fire stream of words from which Gina understood only "*papa.*"

Papa—Pasquale—addressed his son with a few words, but Rocco didn't respond so Pasquale turned to the familiar customer. He knew that a good businessman in America always made his customers feel welcome, at least that's what his wife, Angelina, had translated for him in the English language book. So he gave Gina a big smile and said "hello!" and then turned his back on all of them and began emptying the box onto the counter next to a large wooden cutting board. There was something comical about the older guy, something Gina liked but couldn't quite put her finger on. But he never interacted with her other than his oddly placed hellos.

Rocco began to whistle as he took the pizza box and opened it. He looked over at Gina.

"No more of that red hair. It's good. I like it—your hair. It's nice."

Pasquale heaved a sigh and began slicing the onions.

Gina absently felt the strands of closely cropped hair on the side of her head. She pulled a short piece behind her ear and asked Patrice. "He doesn't wear a wedding ring? Is it because he's at work?"

Patrice was wiping the work area with a wet cloth. "Stay away from my brother, *Jane*." She said it with a smile and it was meant to be silly banter—like Rocco's sweet sounding flirtations—but she was not as adept as Rocco when it came to deceit. And anyway, she really meant it. She smiled again and looked at her brother.

"I hear you." Rocco was looking at Gina. He closed the pizza box again. "I'm not married. I'm all yours." He sang as he came around the counter and handed her the box just as she stood up and then he bowed to her and Gina took the box, too tongue-tied to answer.

As Gina walked out the door, Patrice said, "He's not married because he spent ten years in jail. It's hard to find a wife when you go away at fifteen."

Gina's heart banged against her ribcage as she took in that information. "*Fifteen? He's twenty-five? Ten years between us. Geez. He looks older.*" The jail-part barely registered in her mind and it should have, especially after what had happened to her father. The conversation continued between Rocco and Patrice after Gina was far from earshot and they watched her walk to her car.

"Why are you interfering?" Rocco said to his sister in English so his father would not understand. He hit his hand down hard onto the wooden counter, just as their mother, Angelina, emerged from the back room.

He said to his sister, "If you don't like it, stay out of it."

"Like what?" Angelina asked. A customer waiting for his pizza was wondering the same but Angelina smiled at him and said, "Are you being helped?"

"Of course, Mama." Patrice answered as she moved toward the pizza oven and opened the door.

"What's going on, Pat?" Angelina said quietly to her husband in Italian. She never used his full name, Pasquale. That was only for official papers—like immigration.

"I don't know." He shrugged.

Of course he didn't know. He didn't speak a lick of English, except for a few niceties he'd picked up around the store. Despite the fact he'd married *her*, the only English teacher on their small island, despite the fact that she'd taught their own children the language and tried time and time again to teach him, despite the fact that he'd been in the United States for almost two years, he still understood almost nothing. What had she expected? He barely knew his own language. He was a shepherd after all. Well, maybe not by choice, but it had been a good alternative when the ironworks shop was destroyed. But even in his iron shop, with the noise of the furnace and the banging metal, he'd never been much of a talker. But with those goats—spending his days alone on the mountain peak with no one to talk to but them. What had she expected?

It was his idea to come to this place—America! To save Rocco. She'd wanted England—there were friends that could help them get settled, but no—Pasquale insisted on America. His rich cousin had a store—but they had to hurry and then Rocco's visa was denied.

She heaved a sigh. Her back still ached from the seven-hour airplane ride that she'd just returned from and all that bending over the sink in the back room didn't help it much. How was she, an only child, supposed to help her aging parents alone on the island when there was an ocean between them? Travelling back and forth and working the hours in this pizzeria—another long sigh—it was impossible. There was no point in thinking about it now, though. The dinner rush was getting underway.

*   *   *   *

Gina fiddled with the top of the pizza box as she pulled onto the main road. Her house was just around the corner from the pizzeria, but she wasn't quite ready to go home. The trees were just starting to awaken in the mid-April sun and their boughs with the tiny bead-like buds had a slight greenish haze that could be seen only when the slant of light was just right.

With one hand on the steering wheel, she pulled one of the round muddy-red slices of pepperoni from the hot cheese and tossed it out the window—and then another, and another. A few of them were caught by the breeze and stuck to the car door.

She barely noticed the sign with its painted gold letters as it passed her by on the side of the road. *Leaving Robin's Nest.* But she did see the traffic on the other side of the narrow country road. That was unusual—traffic.

"There must be an accident or something," she thought, but she hadn't passed one. Maybe she hadn't noticed it as she was picking at the pepperoni. *"Maybe it's that construction at the crossroads in town."*

She made a mental note to return home by the back roads as she gingerly pushed her hand under one slice of pizza, ready to pull it to her mouth but it was hot—too hot. She burned her fingertips and pulled them away but the pizza came with them and landed cheese down on the console between the front seats.

Damn!

The police officer behind the row of maple trees was looking intently into the radar gun's output numbers when he heard the honk and looked up to see Gina's car swerving out of the lane, narrowly missing a small pickup truck on the opposite side. Naturally, he pulled his squad car out onto the road in pursuit—if *pursuit* can be categorized as a short thirty-mile-per-hour roll.

The cheese and sauce were dripping down into the gear shifter and Gina really did not want to push the stick into *park* as she pulled to the side of the road. It would just mash everything further down into the holes and crevices and it would be impossible to clean. So she kept her foot pressed down on the brake pedal as she tried to pull some of the melted cheese from the gear shifter but she didn't quite have that kind of coordination. It was sort of like trying to rub your stomach while you pat your head.

Her car began to roll a bit as her foot unconsciously pulled up from the brake. She heard yelling from behind the car and looked in the rearview mirror to see a police hat with two squinting eyes below its rim, jogging after the car. It all happened in a few seconds. She pushed her foot down hard, shocked at the fact that the car was actually moving and then she heard a thud as the officer hit the back of the car and limped to her side window with his hand on his gun and a scowl on his face.

"Gina?" He let out a long loud sigh, "Are you out of your mind?"

Geez. Sometimes she felt like a character in a 1950s sitcom. The police officer was her husband's friend, Lucas.

"Are you high or something?" He asked it as though expecting an answer. He lowered his head and his eyes darted from the open pizza box to the gooey mess of cheese and sauce dripping from the gear shifter. And at that moment her cell phone rang in her bag and then the ringing shifted to her dashboard as the Bluetooth took over. She looked up at Lucas.

"Go ahead." He said.

Gina pushed the button on the steering wheel and said, "Hello?"

"Gina?" the voice was familiar to both of them. "Where are you? I got home early and the T.V. is on and you're—"

"I'm just picking up a pizza, Joe."

The officer interjected. "Yeah—I just pulled her over."

"Who is that? Lucas, is that you? What's going on?"

"Nothing—your wife is on her way home. She'll tell you when she gets there."

Gina shook her head slowly and closed the pizza box. She couldn't think of anything to say. "I'll talk to you in a little while, Joe. I'll be home in fifteen."

Then she pressed the button on the steering wheel again and Joe was gone.

"Nino's Pizza?" Lucas was reading the box. His eyebrows

crunched into a puzzled mass of bushy black hair. He looked at Gina and hit the top of the car, just above her head.

"Drive safely, Gina," he said as he turned and walked back to his patrol car.

Gina watched him through her rearview mirror. She saw him sit behind the steering wheel and she waited but he just continued watching her so she put her car in drive and waited for a chance to pull back onto the road. And just as the wheels of her sedan got traction on the gravel, she glanced quickly into the rearview mirror one last time and saw Lucas holding a cell phone to his ear.

Joe was waiting for her at the door when she pulled the car around the corner and headed straight down White Picket Lane. She saw his large shadow behind the screen the minute she turned the corner. She drove a bit slower than usual, watching the shadow become Joe as he opened the screen door and walked out onto the front porch.

The oak tree that had been struck by lightening the summer before stretched out its broken limb like an eagle without a wing. Joe reached for it and brushed the bark with his hand as he walked down the porch steps and watched Gina pull into the driveway. The car came to a stop just outside the garage. Joe reached for the driver's door as Gina fiddled with the pizza box, closing it and pulling it off the front passenger seat. A wet greasy film soaked into the upholstery. Joe opened the door with one hand while peeling a piece of pepperoni from the side of the car. He looked at it momentarily before tossing it onto the well-manicured lawn.

"Pizza," Gina said as she handed him the box and he took it but also waited for her to collect her bag from the car floor before answering.

"Gina, there's a pot of rice on the stove."

"Yeah." She knew she needed a story that would make some kind of sense—about the pizza, the mess in the car, the television that she'd left on, the rice—but nothing came to her and she was tired of trying.

"You didn't come to work today," Joe said.

"I felt sick, right after you left."

It was true. She *had* felt sick—a bit nauseous. She'd thought maybe, just maybe, it might be morning sickness—and then that which had been in the forefront of all her hopes since marrying Joe, ten years before, was suddenly a bad thing, an unwanted thing—something that would tie them together forever and would need a competent lucid mother, qualities she knew she lacked. And suddenly the nausea terrified her.

"How come you didn't pick up when I called?" Joe persisted. "I was worried."

"I was sick—I told you—didn't feel good." Gina walked past him into the house.

"Gina," Joe started softly, "It's your father?" It was half question and half suggestion. "Maybe you should see someone."

"*Yeah,*" Gina thought, "*There is someone.*" But she said to Joe, "Maybe you're right."

Of course it had affected her—her father being one of the victims of the Dunmore prison break, the coverage in the press reaching every inch of the globe—a globe that had the circumference of a large beach ball in Gina's eyes. Her idea of the world was built upon the distant memory of a small plastic globe from elementary school. But people as far as Japan watched as the saga unfolded on BBC world news via satellite. Two escaped convicts in New Jersey, a tunnel found inside a prison cell. It was like the plot of an unrealistic adventure movie or a melodramatic paperback and yet it was real life, a story with more fire than any reporter could have hoped.

"Inside help," said the faces behind the microphones as they stood in front of bright yellow police tape. A female guard had been persuaded to be the getaway driver, her story slowly unfolding in emails and handwritten notes in the days after the escape. Her body was discovered in her car with the discarded prison kakis of the two fugitives. The world watched for a week before the SWAT team finally closed in on the ill-fated hunting lodge.

Gina 's father was as stubborn as cold maple syrup and he had insisted on going into the west woods to secure his cabin—the entrance had never had a lock on it and now that the fugitives had made it down there, he was determined to put one on—though Gina and her mother could not make him see the warped logic of deterring criminals with a locked door.

Gina thought of the photos in the newspaper, clippings her mother had obsessively collected—those prisoners' faces—black and white mug shots. *Prisoners* from *prison*. Was that the same as jail? Patrice had said *jail*, not prison. That's different. Only petty criminals go to jail—marijuana smokers and jay walkers—but ten years? For a fifteen-year-old boy? That's a long time. Maybe Italy had stricter laws.

When the police identified her father, the grief Gina had felt over the loss was so sudden, that every unkind word between them, every pointless argument, every question she'd delayed asking, came flooding back in a tidal wave of grief. It was a grief that subsided and then hid in the shadows, appearing later at the most unlikely of times. But it was a grief that should have reared its head when she'd heard of Rocco's past, though that same heavy sadness may have been that which had led her to Rocco in the first place. After all, his accent, his aggressive way—those were her father's—though they were always qualities she'd disliked.

Gina turned toward the pot on the cold stove and picked it up by the handle. She looked at the white rice inside and then looked at Joe who was watching her closely and then put it back on the unlit burner.

"I'll call someone, tomorrow," she said, mostly because she didn't know what else to say, and that usually seemed to please him and what she really wanted to say—*get out of here. I can't stand your face* — clearly was too cruel and unwarranted.

It wasn't hate she felt, so much as suffocation — like a cloud of smoke that needed to be batted from her face so she could breath and so she could see more clearly what lay ahead. No maybe not suffocation, that was a bit too dramatic. Maybe frustration, but that didn't really conjure up quite the sense of what was simmering inside her — something like fatigue or weariness. Well, the truth was, though she had volumes of dictionary words in her head, none of them seemed to explain the heaviness of her limbs that prevented her from moving forward.

And a few days later, she was in the pizzeria again.

CHAPTER 3

"Still no answer," Angelina put the telephone back on the coffee table. She was sitting with Pasquale in the living area of the apartment over the pizzeria as the light of dawn fought the dust on the window panes. Below the window sat a table small enough to hold a hot plate and toaster-oven but big enough for a waist-high refrigerator to fit underneath it. Next to the table were two old cabinets with a slab of wood that provided a flat surface for a makeshift counter.

"Call Maria and Big Antonio," Pasquale said, "Your mother is always up there visiting with them."

"I have. No answer there either. Remind me later to call again, before it gets too late over there." But Angelina needed no reminder. There was hardly a moment when the guilt of leaving her mother with such a burden was not weighing on her.

"Hm." Pasquale slowly stood from the sofa as he put his coffee cup down on the table in front of it. He began to fold the blankets, though it was more like rolling them in a ball.

"Let me," Angelina stood up and walked over to him grabbing the side of one blanket and smoothing it out in front of her, using her torso as a flat surface. "Pasquale, there's plenty of room to sleep next to Rocco in the bedroom."

"Agh! He snores." Pasquale said, but thought, "*I miss you.*"

18

Angelina laid the folded blanket back on the sofa. "We can afford a bigger apartment. Three bedrooms."

"No. No." He shook his head. "The money is for Rocco. For when we leave—it will help him. It's hard to run the place by himself."

"If we move from here, we can rent it out." Move back home, is what she was thinking and of her daughter who was lost in limbo because of Rocco's mistakes. "Patrice deserves a life, Pasquale. If not here, then back home."

"Not this again." He'd meant it as a thought, but it escaped as spoken words.

Angelina let out a sigh—too loud to be called a sigh—with enough anger behind it, to start an engine.

"I understand," she said, her voice punching the air, "But we cannot sacrifice Patrice—or my parents. He can do it. Javier can help him. Give Javier half ownership or at least consider his offer. That money could get us home and Rocco would have the help he needs."

Angelina moved too quickly in the small space and as she turned to walk away, she hit her leg on the coffee table. She bent to rub her leg, her eyes blazing at Pasquale with what she'd have described as *hate* if someone had interrupted the moment to ask. But hate lay beside love, sometimes indistinguishable.

"You okay?" Pasquale went to her but she pushed him away.

The door near the hotplate opened and Patrice emerged with her hair a mass of tangles and sleep in her eyes.

"I didn't hear you get out of bed," she was looking at her mother. "Is the bathroom free?"

Without waiting for an answer, she shuffled across the small living area and closed the bathroom door behind her.

"I'm going for a walk." Angelina said to Pasquale. "You start the pizza ovens."

Out in the empty parking lot among the small chickadees that flew between the maples near the street, Angelina let out a long exhale until the apartment air was free of her lungs. She decided on a direction and then started out with a brisk stride along the cracked sidewalk. She turned a corner and the cement below her feet became perfect gray squares. She was inside a neighborhood.

That morning, from the apartment window, she'd looked out over the budding branches of the maples that sat in front of the tall wooden fence. Through their boughs, she had seen the roofs behind the store, the same roofs she'd been looking at for eighteen months, wondering about the houses below those roofs, about the families inside, but this was the first time she'd followed the curve of the sidewalk rather than continue on the main avenue.

The houses were in a tight row so from the sidewalk one looked as though it were an addition of the next. Only on closer examination as the perfect sidewalk squares progressed, could the small space between each house be seen. It was a space small enough for someone standing at a window of one house to throw an object into the window of the next. But the space was a clear division of territory.

Angelina's thoughts kept her from really seeing the houses or the squirrels scurrying up the tree trunks that lined the street as she passed by each. They were no more than a mix of colors in her peripheral vision. A small brown dog with a gigantic-dog's bark ran from the shade of an azalea bush and along his fenced-in yard, waking Angelina from her reverie just long enough for her to register that he was unable to get to her as he ran back and forth behind the chain-links. He was not so much protecting his territory as begging for escape — until Angelina disappeared behind the shrubs that bordered the next house and he slinked back to his place in the shade.

This was not what Angelina had expected in America, not at all how Pasquale had described it. Their children were supposed to have a *better* life. Rocco was going to escape the damaged name he'd made for himself but instead he'd traded one jail cell for another with his family joining him. The days were spent on the bottom of the store, the nights, on the top. They barely breathed the outdoor air. And the sea — oh the sea! She dearly missed her island home with the sea's sparkle, mirrored against the mountain ridge. The American sea with its angry gray mass of turbulence was so unlike the one at home and it was a twenty-minute car ride from the pizzeria — so far away, it may as well not have existed.

This was not at all what she'd expected when Pasquale had left their island with the money from the sale of the herd. Not at all what she'd expected when she and Patrice had come over. Nor what she'd expected for Rocco who had to sneak into the country like the criminal he was. Now the money from the sale of the goats was gone and instead they had Cousin Nino's store in a place where the people lived in tight little rows, in houses with closed windows and closed doors.

An odd oak tree caught Angelina's attention. One large limb appeared to have broken off leaving a jagged appendage where it had once been. She'd always fancied herself a bit of a poet and thought, *"that's us, rooted in this place but broken."*

She smiled at her wit and then felt a jolt to her hip that knocked all the air from her lungs as she landed in the street. She hadn't seen the car as it slowly backed down the driveway. The driver's voice came from the open car window.

"Oh my God!" It was a woman's voice.

Angelina put her hands in the street, ready to pick herself off the pavement but two fuzzy blue slippers appeared next to her and she looked up to see an old man in pajamas. It seemed that he should have been there to aid her, but he was looking over her head and reprimanding.

"Good God, Gina! You could have killed her."

"I know. I know. I'm so sorry."

The driver had swung the car door open and was running around to the back bumper. Angelina watched her perfectly white sneakers approach and then looked up to see blue — lots of blue, a blue shirt and blue pants but the sun was in her eyes so she looked away. Both the driver and the pajama-man tried to help Angelina to her feet. But they weren't quite coordinated as they pulled at her and she swayed a bit, giving the mistaken impression of being hurt more than she actually was. And the blood that dripped off her elbow wasn't helping matters.

"I'll call the police." It was a different voice now, from behind. "They'll get an ambulance.

"The police? Oh God—no!" Angelina thought and then quickly said, "I'm fine. Really. I just need a minute."

Again, Gina said, "I'm so sorry," and at that moment she met Angelina's gaze and they were both struck with the same look of recognition. Gina felt as if her heart could not pound any louder without knocking her unconscious.

She said, "I-I-I can drive you to the hospital. I'm on my way there."

"To the hospital?" Angelina asked. Her eyebrows pulled together in confusion, "You're going to the hospital?"

She knew this face.

"To work. Yes."

"Oh." Angelina said, "No, no. I'm fine."

"The hospital for a few scrapes and bruises?" It seemed extreme.

The voice from behind became the plump face of a man in a business suit. "You should go. Just in case." He offered this advice as he walked back to his yard—the one with the barking dog.

The fuzzy slippers began to retreat across the street and the two women were left alone.

"Really, I'm fine. *Jane*, is it?" Angelina asked.

"Actually, Gina."

"Oh, hmm." Angelina was confused. Perhaps she'd been injured a bit more than she'd realized. "Maybe I should just sit for a second." She was lowering herself to the curb when Gina grabbed her uninjured elbow.

"No—please come in and let me at least wash and dress your elbow. You really are hurt."

Angelina *did* want to see inside the house. She hadn't been inside any American houses yet, but this woman's house, in particular, interested her. She was curious.

"Let me just pull the car back up into the driveway," Gina said as she made her way to the driver's side of the car with Angelina standing, watching, holding her arm.

The kitchen had the aroma of warm bread and dishwasher soap. Gina led Angelina to the sink and ran cool water over her battered elbow. Then Angelina sat on a bar stool and looked around. From where she sat at the kitchen counter, she could see the entire living area and near the front door where the railing of a stairway led to a second floor.

"Are you a doctor?" Angelina asked, the light from the window alit in her eyes as she looked at Gina's blue scrubs.

Gina smiled, "A speech pathologist." She was patting Angelina's arm with a dry towel and feeling a bit calmer. "You work at the pizzeria around the corner, don't you?"

"We own it. My family—my husband." A buzzing noise stopped her as Gina reached into one of her shirt pockets, pulled out a phone, looked at it briefly with a scowl and returned it to the pocket.

"You'll be late for work." Angelina said.

Gina shrugged.

"I see you at the store often. You like pizza a lot." This was the woman Rocco often flirted with. Angelina was sure. She had wanted to talk to her for a long time—away from Rocco and now here she was.

"I hear my daughter call you Jane?" It was half a question.

"Patrice is your daughter?"

"Yes. Jane? Gina?"

Gina heaved a sigh that momentarily raised her chest. "Well, I didn't correct her the first time she said it. It didn't seem important. I hadn't expected to come back." Gina was walking around her kitchen, gathering scissors and tape from different drawers that she left open as she walked across the living area to a door Angelina guessed to be a bathroom.

"Oh," Gina looked back at Angelina as she turned the doorknob. "It's not that I, well yes. I was going to come back again because your store—it's uh, very nice, good pizza. I just didn't think it would matter. The name I mean."

There was another loud sigh as Gina ducked into the bathroom and immerged with a roll of gauze and a small tube of something. Gina continued as she laid the materials out on the counter.

"It just didn't seem important at that moment and then Patrice kept using that name—calling me Jane. I thought she would have just forgotten it. And well, after so much time went by, it felt odd to correct her—it would be weird—to correct an error after so much time. You kind of end up saying, okay, so the mistake was made, but I can live with it, correcting it now would mean I'd have to explain like I'm doing with you, right? You get it? I just accepted it even though it was wrong—not really who I am. Too much time went by, too late to change. You know what I mean?"

Angelina put her head down and looked at her feet on the rung of the stool.

"Actually I do," she said quietly.

"Your English is really good." Gina said.

"I studied in England for a year." Angelina held her elbow toward Gina as she applied a salve, and Angelina winced.

"Sorry," Gina looked up. "But you're not from England. Your Italian, right?"

"Yes, of course," Angelina said. "You like our pizza?" She remembered why she'd wanted to talk to Gina. She tried again. "You come there a lot. It's the pizza?"

"Yeah. It's good."

Gina's reddened face did not go unnoticed. Angelina continued, "You like Rocco?"

Gina felt like a child caught with her hand in the cookie jar. She held her breath for a moment and then said, "he seems like a nice guy."

Her face felt as if it were sunburnt. The kitchen was hot. She walked to the window and pulled the shade down, blocking the light. Then she went back to Angelina and picked up the gauze.

"Who's in that photo?" Angelina had craned her neck around and was looking past the back of the sofa, at the mantle over the fireplace. She'd noticed the wedding picture the moment she'd walked in. "That's you, right?"

Gina's voice had the slightest quiver to it. "Yep, that's me."

Her heart began to bang wildly again, and she quickly wrapped a strip of gauze around Angelina's elbow with such imprecision it became a lumpy rag. She cleared her throat, cut the gauze and taped it. Then she patted the top of the gauzed arm as if it were a child's head.

"Alright then. There you go." It was clearly a signal for Angelina to say her goodbyes and leave. But Angelina was not finished.

"It's a lovely photo. Where's your husband now?"

Dead? Divorced?

"Uh—he's at work. The hospital. He works there too, with me, together—we work. A nurse—he's a nurse. I—uh, I have to go." Gina moved toward the hallway. "To work."

"Yes," said Angelina as she lifted herself from the stool without lifting her eyes from Gina.

But Gina kept her eyes on the rumpled hallway rug and absently bent down to straighten it out.

"I guess your husband likes pizza too, then," Angelina said.

Your husband, your husband, your husband. You have a husband.

"Yeah," Gina said. It followed a quiet laugh, the one that always appeared when she was nervous.

Angelina followed her down the hallway and looked up the staircase as she exited the screen door that Gina was holding open. Angelina held the door open for Gina, assuming she'd follow but Gina pulled the door closed and remained on the other side of it. She watched as Angelina walked down the driveway. Then Angelina turned back briefly and gave her a little nod, lifting her bandaged arm — a weak good-bye. Gina backed away from the screen door until her heel brushed against the bottom stair of the staircase and she slowly lowered herself to it and sat.

The telephone rang on the wall in the kitchen. Gina gasped and jumped up to answer it. She was half way down the hall when she bent over and vomited on the neatly straightened rug.

Angelina was walking past the barking dog when she looked down at the mess of gauze and tape Gina had made. It looked as if it were a broken arm or at least a gaping wound, with white gauze wrapped half way up her arm. As she walked around the curve and back onto the main avenue, she picked at the tape with her thumb and forefinger.

Pasquale paced the floor of the pizzeria, a carving knife in his hand and an apron dripping with the guts of tomatoes. He saw Angelina just as the tape pulled free and she began unraveling the mummy-like gauze from her arm. She was dumping it in the town trash can at the mouth of the parking lot when he ran to the door of the store, forgetting he hadn't unlocked it yet, smashing into the window — momentarily dazed. Angelina saw the knife and what she thought was blood on his apron and ran to him.

"Open the door!" she shouted in such a panic, Pasquale could barely find the lever as he watched the blood ooze from her elbow. Her arms were up and her hands were in two tight fists, the sick feeling in her gut beginning to subside as she recognized the red tomato stains and put her arms down.

"Oh Pat," she said when the door no longer separated them. "Tomatoes." She shook her head and touched his arm.

"Who did this to you?" He was still holding the knife and looking past her wildly.

"It's a scrape. I fell."

Pasquale was scanning the parking lot with tiger eyes, the knife gripped tightly at his side. He had the protective testosterone stance that he'd brought with him from his island, though he was slowly realizing his impotence among the English speakers of this new territory. He knew, however, this was one situation he was prepared to resolve—no words needed, just the knife whose handle was now part of his fist.

"I was walking in the neighborhood behind the store and I didn't see a car backing out from one of the houses. It bumped me and I fell. It's nothing."

"A car?" His eyes again scanning as he closed the door behind them and flipped the lock.

"Pat, it was the one we talked about, the girl."

"The blue-sedan girl? She hit you with her car?"

"I told you it was an accident. I wasn't watching and—"

"Well, she wasn't watching either." Pasquale took hold of Angelina's forearm and gently twisted his head to see her elbow.

"She was backing her car from the front of her house." Angelina continued. "She lives right behind here." She nodded her head at the back kitchen door. "You can see our apartment window from her kitchen."

"She invited you in? She hit you with her car and then invited you in?"

"I told you," Angelina sighed, "it was an accident." Angelina hung on the last word. She pulled her arm from Pasquale's grasp and looked at him.

"She's married, Pat. She has a husband."

"No." Pasquale whispered. "Then where the devil is he?"

"There in the house. I didn't see him, but I saw a wedding photo and she told me they work together. I didn't quite understand what she said, but I think she's a doctor."

Pasquale gulped. "What do you mean you didn't understand her?"

Angelina had perfect English. She'd been to England. She'd taught English on the island. She was supposed to be his lifeline, here in this temporary place. "Why not? Too fast? Maybe she was—"

"No, I understood her but her job was pathologist-something. I didn't catch it. That's all. Anyway—that's why she brought me into her house. To help me."

"After she hit you with her car."

"Yes—but there's a husband, a smiling one, in a photo. It's no good, Pat."

"No good." Pasquale looked down at his knife and nodded.

CHAPTER 4

Incompresso was a small fishing village on a forgotten island, an island that lay just at the heel of Italy's boot, as if it were about to be crushed like an unnoticed insect underfoot. And on that island, Giovanna Boeri continued to wait for word of her daughter's return.

Giovanna's house, sat at the foot of the only mountain on the island, in fact the mountain *was* the island, a jagged rock pushing up through the sea.

The house was tucked so far into the mountain's lap, the bedroom window at the back of the house had a wall of dirt and rocks only a few meters from the shutters. Giovanna was constantly shooing the insects and frogs away from the windowsill as they came to rest in the shade.

Incompresso's one jagged peak provided a flow of spring water that fell straight down from a high ledge where the smallest twinkle of water could be seen as it cascaded from the top. It broke into a river making its way to less vertical landscape, and then flowed along the upper pasture and down through the middle of the village.

The stone bridge over the river was made long before memory. Its arched back rose above a trickling riverbed in late summer and a rushing torrent in the spring. It was a majestic bridge at one time, wide enough for two mules to pass each other without incident, but nowadays when two cars were trying to cross it at the same time, one had to wait while the other crossed over. It was over that bridge, that Giovanna's husband, Pastore di Capre, would walk up to the plateau where the green grass dried to the color of honey and the view of the sea was endless. That's where his goat shed now stood empty and forgotten—all of the goats having been sold or butchered to fund his son-in-law's move to America.

Incompresso did not hold any mines of gold. Its sharp-edged coastline offered no tourist beaches or hotel plots and it was too small for a strategically placed military base of modern times. Thus, since the long-gone days of kingdoms and castles, the island had been left to its own devices, which Giovanna, like most others of her generation had always felt was a bit of good fortune. Through wars and famine and political upheaval, their tiny island was mostly left untouched. And so, to Giovanna, Incompresso was a place that remained a safe haven in a dangerous world, a place one should never want to leave.

And yet they did—they left in droves, especially after the lira were exchanged for euros. The young people, never having experience war or fear of invasion, equated Incompresso's isolation with confinement. They could no longer make a living in the sea as the fish dwindled and the world's plastic debris washed ashore.

The route to *civilization* was on the small ferry that ran once a day from the heel of the mainland—if the water was calm enough for passage. The privately owned boats of Incompresso were many, but they were small ill-equipped fishing boats, so the ferry was the vessel on which one could reliably sail to Mother Italia and dock safely at a mainland port.

Giovanna's son-in-law, Pasquale—Pat—had said he'd have Angelina back within the year—just as soon as young Rocco could take over, but Giovanna was getting impatient. Her husband,

Pastore di Capre, needed constant care and God knows she wasn't getting any younger. None of it made sense to her.

Twenty-six years before, when Pasquale had come to ask for the hand of Angelina, their only child, Pastore di Capre had been as thrilled as she for Pasquale was one who would surely not leave the island. Like most of the young men, he was the son of a fisherman.

Well, actually, when he asked for Angelina's hand one might say he was a blacksmith, but to Pastore di Capre and everyone else on the island—except perhaps Angelina—ironwork was a pastime not something with which to feed one's family, which Pasquale proved time and time again when he would not charge a fee to those he knew, and he knew everyone on the island. So his father's fishing boat had been the true source of their livelihood and in those earlier years it had been the most productive vessel on Incompresso. For that reason, Giovanna and her husband had been quite happy with the prospect of Pasquale becoming their new son-in-law.

Pasquale had sailed with his father, Old Rocco, every morning before dawn since he was old enough to lift the fishing nets. And after the frozen-fish story ran in the big Italian newspaper back in the 1960s, the mainlanders wanted only fish from Old Rocco's catch, which made him a rich man and his son, Pasquale, an even better catch for Giovanna's daughter.

Back then the ferry came twice a day, just after sunrise and a little after noon. It docked near the tavern, which at that time was no more than a small square box made of grey stones that housed a few tables. Over the years, the tavern owner made some changes, but not many. When indoor plumbing came to the island he added a small three-stool bar area with a sink. And the outdoor *bathroom* became a storeroom while the tavern owner placed a small porcelain toilet and tiny sink in an attached room that he called a water closet. He himself piled the cinderblocks and smoothed the walls of the small room near the back door, the floor remaining a mix of dirt and rock, as he never quite saw the need to spruce up an area that he'd be hosing down with his new outdoor spigot and long black tubing he'd bought on the mainland. But it was under the portico roof that most patrons spent their time. Its corrugated tin sat atop two stone pillars and hung from the tavern entrance making a formidable sitting area with several metal tables and a mix of wooden chairs. And it was at one of those tables under that portico roof, at the entrance of the tavern that the ferry captain could be found in those early days as he waited for his crew to prepare for the return to the mainland.

Mostly though, the ferry brought the villagers off the island to get supplies from the port on the other side. It rarely carried a car in its cargo hold unless the doctor was making his monthly visit.

But for a long time, it carried some of the buyers from the mainland restaurants who sought out Old Rocco and rarely bothered with the other fishermen. They called themselves buyers. It had an official ring to it, but most were family members of the restaurant owner or low-paid managers, or an occasional enterprising waiter who might take up the task with the hope of pocketing something on the side.

The first newspaper story brought them to Incompresso but it was the second that brought them to Old Rocco. One investigative reporter had heard a rumor about the fishing habits on the mainland's southern coast. He traveled down Italy's calf, posing as a dock worker, to turn the frozen-fish rumor to fact and in doing so destroyed the livelihood of hundreds and set other reporters in action. The story said that those mainland fishermen were buying frozen fish and passing it off as their own — freshly caught.

Fishing can be physically grueling and somewhat stressful, especially when a restaurateur is preordering what hasn't yet been caught. So there probably was some truth to the story, but unfortunately for the honest fishermen, that reputation along their coast hurt everyone. They could still fish for their families but the restaurateurs—or more accurately, the customers in the restaurants—wanted fish from the island fishermen.

Old Rocco—Pasquale's father—was quoted in the second news story written by that same adventurous reporter who had hoped to be a novelist but had settled for newspaper writing and the notoriety it had given him with the frozen-fish story. It was from Old Rocco that everyone on the mainland wanted fresh fish, after reading or hearing about his quoted statement.

You see, as the frozen-fish story began to peter out, that same reporter searched for something new. It's a difficult world to inhabit after one's work has been held up and admired. And there was still a competitive newspaper market that had a few hundred Italian newspapers rolling off the presses every day. So that reporter came to the island with a rented boat and a borrowed camera. He sat with the tavern owner, enjoying the local grappa, pining for the beauty of an island that tugged at his imagination—and with each sip, as the grappa loosened his tongue a bit, he confessed his desire to be an author in search of a muse, rather than the reporter he'd become. The tavern owner paid no attention and kept his glass full. The reporter needed to make a living so he continued writing on his notepad as he sat in the shade of the portico roof at the front of the tavern.

Old Rocco happened to have stopped by to exchange some of his fish for the tavern owner's garden tomatoes. He sat with the reporter for a few minutes while the tavern owner ruffled around in his back storeroom looking for a sack. The resulting newspaper article filled with description and longing, carried Old Rocco's wise and intellectual words to all of its readers in Italy.

It said: "*Unlike those on the mainland, here we are cerebral fishermen. We use our minds and intellect to find the schools and lure them into our nets. We would never think of deceiving anyone with frozen fish.*"

When the newspaper came on the ferry a few days later, Pasquale's father needed the article read to him and when his son got to the part with his quote—or more appropriately, his misquote—Old Rocco asked, "What does *cerebral* mean?"

Pasquale explained it as best he could as he thumbed through the worn-out dictionary from the schoolhouse, "Smart, I guess." There were other words but that was the one Pasquale chose. He was always interested in the most direct and efficient way. "Cerebral means smart."

His father nodded his head slowly.

"I like it," Old Rocco said as he smiled and thought, "*It doesn't make sense; fishing is about strength and patience, but I like it. Cerebral. Smart.*" He looked up at his son and nodded his head. "Cerebral—that's good."

So for a short while the forgotten island was remembered. If the ferry arrived before Old Rocco returned with his boat, the buyers would mill around the other returning fishing boats, watching the men roll the nets, making small talk and buying a fish here or there so as to remain amiable and welcome guests in a place they knew only as the fish island. But if Pasquale and his father returned to the dock before the ferry landed, the fish buyers would seek him out at the tavern or at his home. The smallness of the island made it an easy guess as to where he'd be.

They'd buy as much as Old Rocco would allow. Then they'd pack it in the large tubs they'd brought with them and eat a meal under the tavern's portico roof while awaiting the noon ferry in which a container of ice would be provided for their purchased fish, only to return the next day to repeat it all again.

The other fishermen resented Old Rocco. But it was actually those mainland restaurateurs who were also responsible for the much-needed medical center on the island, and for that, the villagers were all grateful—even the other fishermen.

On one particular afternoon, one of the buyers who usually came to the island aboard the ferry, sailed into port in his own fancy motorboat. Well, actually it belonged to the owner of the restaurant for whom he bought his fish. The owner had come along to see the island, meet the fishermen, and see how business was done, generally speaking. That's what he told everyone. In fact, he suspected his buyer was cheating him and having already fired and rehired several buyers, he decided to come along and see if it was something he might want to do himself.

As it turned out — it was not.

The restaurateur came a bit earlier than anyone else that day. He sat in the tavern while his buyer dealt with the unpleasant pleasantries of mixing with the villagers. Because he waited a bit longer than usual, he also drank a bit more than his liver was able to recognize. The local grappa was much stronger than the mainland's and he'd grossly misjudged its effect.

As he paid his bill and made his way toward the harbor, he swayed from side to side which prompted the tavern owner to suggest he wait a while before returning to his boat. But he was like every other drunk person — he had very little awareness of how impaired he was. So he waved off the suggestion and walked along the pier looking for his vessel. The boat had been carefully pulled alongside the pier so he and his buyer could easily hop from pier to stern or — as they did on their arrival — from stern to pier. However, with this one quick leap from land to boat, a drunken misstep caused him to fall between the boat and the pier at the very moment a small wave pushed the sea into the harbor. It was an awful howl that sent half the village to the port.

The event was not entirely grim. The good news was that there were several people to pull him from the water before he was crushed. And he barely felt the true pain of the ordeal in his drunken state. The bad news was that the gaping wound in his leg would not stop bleeding so his buyer did what he thought was correct, despite the protests of several fishermen, and a few old women. He tied a belt above the wound, cutting the blood flow, just as he'd seen it done in war movies. By the time the injured restaurateur got back to the mainland and to the nearest medical facility, there was nothing left to do but take the damaged portion of the leg—from the knee down. The tragedy was a news story, once again highlighting the little island and the result was a small medical center manned by several nurses and one medical student, the medical student having been obligated to serve time in a small village before receiving his license from the state.

Back then, it was rare for the medical student—doctor—to have any real patients on the island. And he could often be found at the tavern, conversing with whomever happened by that day—biding his time until he'd be replaced and returned to the mainland.

In the meantime, Old Rocco's fishing boat continued to thrive. It made him a rich man, as rich as his small boat would allow, rich enough to have such a title in a changing world that left the island behind in memories of post-war hunger. Pastore di Capre and Giovanna could not forget those lean times or believe they were gone for good. It's true that they had their own small herd of goats, but it was dwindling and Pastore di Capre was more and more fatigued with climbing the ridge to the pasture. So when Pasquale came to ask for Angelina's hand, Giovanna and Pastore di Capre discussed it and decided that a woman who married into Old Rocco's family would never be hungry—nor would her parents.

And so long after the reporters were forgotten and the ferry service was cut to once a day, the wedding was arranged. Both Pasquale and Angelina were overjoyed by the outcome of the plans they'd devised and the script Angelina had carefully sculpted for Pasquale's conversation with her father, their love already having been consummated atop the ironwork's bench.

Pasquale continued with his ironwork and Angelina encouraged him as she thought he had a talent for it and the workroom bench was the only place they had any privacy now that they were living with his parents.

The birth of their first child coincided with the deadly earthquake off the coast that drowned Old Rocco as he tried to tie his boat to the pier just as the first wave hit and flooded the harbor. The earth trembled in sickening bouts of destruction, until those who were not crushed by the stones of their own homes, had run across the old bridge and made their way to the upper pasture.

Later, through a flood of tears Angelina stood in front of the ironwork's rubble, the workbench broken in two by a large piece of the mountain that had rolled from the peak. Her heart was heavy but her belly was heavier. She turned to Pasquale.

"Pat, what will become of us?" she asked.

And before he could answer, a crushing pain pushed her pelvis and a tiny flood emptied from between her legs. Little Rocco was born a few hours later amid the rubble and chaos. Everyone agreed—it was a happy event, new life rather than more death, but they nodded silently at the thought of being born in such destruction. Only Pastore di Capre and the tavern owner knew the true reason for the quake, for the destruction and for the cursed birth of Pastore di Capre's first-born grandchildren. It was because of Carlo, the foreigner. It was because of his murder. But both the tavern owner and Pastore di Capre would go to their graves without spilling a word of it.

The villagers knew that a birth on such a day would surely come with the *black luck* and follow the poor child throughout his life.

Giovanna was grateful to have lost nothing. Her loved ones were alive, her daughter was safe and the new grandson, little Rocco, had just entered the world. Pastore di Capre forgave them for passing him over when naming the child. He'd been hopeful when he'd found that Pasquale did not have his father's name as was the custom, which of course meant that the new child might be named Pietro, after him—his given name, not his nickname, Pastore di Capre, that he'd acquired after the war. He knew Angelina and Pasquale would weigh the fact that Pastore di Capre did not have any sons to do that for him. But with the death of Old Rocco, so tragically caught in the churning waters of the earthquake, Pastore di Capre completely understood—maybe the next child.

After Old Rocco's fishing boat was gone and the ironworks destroyed, Giovanna and Pastore di Capre worried for the future of their daughter and the baby boy that had come into such a broken world. Pastore di Capre took Pasquale to the upper pasture to teach him about the goats. Pasquale took to it as though he'd been a herder all his life. Perhaps the solitude helped him heal the loss of his father.

It was a difficult time for everyone and reasonable to think that Pastore di Capre began his decline at that time, if one were looking to pinpoint a moment on a timeline as often happens with a person like Pastore di Capre who was losing his hold on the past.

The earthquake, its great flood, the death of Old Rocco—those were not the events that propagated Pastore di Capre's decline, not what Giovanna would say. He'd started his decline before that. It was the day Carlo died. Yes, she knew there was something amiss, but it wasn't her place to question her husband, and well that was the day of her own misfortune that she was trying desperately to accept. But Giovanna remembered the exact moment of her husband's change. He'd come home with blood on his clothes and had stood whispering with the tavern owner in the garden. He was never the same after that, though the changes were too subtle back then for anyone else to see. He was still a young man and it was long before the children wed. In fact, Angelina had not yet been born. But the day Carlo's torn body was brought down from the peak, marked the beginning of Pastore di Capre's slow disappearance.

"He was never the same after Carlo's accident," Giovanna still told people when they asked but there were so few people left who remembered that day or remembered Carlo. Most of the islanders only noticed the changes in Pastore di Capre after his hair had turned to silver-blue and his eyes distant.

Now, Giovanna and Pastore di Capre sat together in two old dining chairs that had found permanent residence in the front yard near the gate. Giovanna looked at her husband, searching for Pietro in his eyes—the man she'd married so long ago. He smiled and for a brief moment he was there—and then gone again. He was slipping away so slowly each day, one miniscule step at a time.

A deep yearning clawed at Giovanna's ribcage, a yearning born of lost opportunity, a yearning to feel his embrace, to look into his eyes and hear his voice deep with certainty. She just wanted a few more hours with him—with her Pietro—to exchange farewells as though he were leaving on a journey but somehow she's missed that moment. Though there really never was such a *moment*. It would have been odd to say goodbye to him while he understood her. Yet now, she felt as though she'd missed his departure and longed for one last moment to feel his arms around her and be swallowed by his warmth.

Those thoughts brought silent tears down her face as she sobbed without making a sound, her shoulders shaking with the rhythm of her sorrow. She bent her head and emptied her heart into her hands.

She was lonelier since her sister-in-law had passed away. Pastore di Capre's sister had never married and had always been a great help to Giovanna. Now, without her and with Pastore di Capre's slow departure, Giovanna had become cold—even on the warmest of days. It was a chill that lived inside her bones and there were no shawls, no fires, no words that could warm her. Without her daughter and her grandchildren nearby, even the warmth of the sun ceased to permeate the walls of her home.

"Angelina, come home," she whispered between sobs and thought, "*Why did the young ones have to leave?*"

The truth was impossible for Giovanna to understand—the reality of the newer world that had swallowed her old one. It was a world from which she was completely excluded, a world in

which her daughter, Angelina, could only live on the periphery—
simply because of her age and proximity to the generation after.
Oh sure, Angelina had one of those small telephones that the kids
worshipped with their heads bent low—their eyes alit from the
blue glow of the screen. Everyone had one.

But Giovanna also saw Angelina struggle with it and knew her
daughter was maybe not as ignorant as she, but certainly not in
possession of the same technical savvy as her granddaughter,
Patrice. Even the smaller children in the village—barely babies—
knew more than Giovanna who was supposed to be enjoying the
age of wisdom and respect her parents had before her. But
somehow something had changed and she had gone from the
ignorant younger generation to the ignorant older generation.
And that just seemed grossly unfair.

Giovanna saw people poking their fingers on tablets, but were
they large telephones or tiny televisions? She wasn't sure and at
first she didn't care. It was only when the tavern owner changed
his sign to read: *Internet Café* that it became too much. What had
he been thinking? No doubt it was his grandson's idea. Now the
quiet tavern was pinging and dinging day and night as patrons—
mostly children after school—sat in front of the computers,
feeding coins into slots. It had become impossible to bring Pastore
di Capre there for a quiet cup of coffee. It confused him and made
him angry. These changes were not good.

"But what do I know," Giovanna thought, *"I'm just an old
woman."*

She had lived her entire eighty-five years on that tiny island
where nothing changed, not even after two wars and an
earthquake, until the recent lightening-speed of what the
television news announcers called technology. She simply could
not comprehend a world where one's image was able to ricochet
between a multitude of towers—one of those towers on the peak
above the village—allowing her to see her daughter standing in a
pizzeria in America!

The tavern owner's grandson never seemed to be deterred by her scowl as he held the small telephone up for her.

"It's a mobile, Nonna Giovanna. This is *Facetime*. " The young man said the same thing every time.

"In America it's called a cell."

"A seal." Giovanna tried the word each time, hopeful as she awaited the connection but the voices were always scratchy and the images froze and unfroze like the television on stormy days. It confused her. When she talked, they talked and no one understood what was being said.

"Call me on the house phone," she'd end up saying as she batted the phone from her face.

The tavern owner's grandson would leave her but he'd try again on a different day, when he'd get another call from Angelina or Patrice. Rocco and Pasquale never called. After a failed Facetime attempt, Giovanna usually ended up sitting patiently by the house telephone — waiting. And when it didn't ring she'd get angry.

The telephone had never been her friend.

The one in the house was difficult enough for her. It had been impossible to get accustomed to when it was installed thirty-odd years earlier. At first they kept the contraption sitting on the floor, unplugged because every time it rattled awake with its loud bell, she'd jump a meter before she understood what it was. And it would always be one of Angelina's friends. Why not just go outside and walk to the person's house? But on the day that Pastore di Capre answered it and it was a boy's voice — well, who could blame him — a boy talking to Angelina, too lazy to come with his feet to their front door and address her parents as was appropriate. Pastore di Capre pulled the cord clear from the wall and the telephone sat unused until almost thirty years later when Angelina had it reinstalled, a few days before she'd left Incompresso to join Pasquale in America.

But Giovanna had been perfectly content getting her telephone calls at Maria's house which sat just a few feet above hers. When a call came for Giovanna, Maria would yell down to her and Giovanna would help Pastore di Capre climb up the path that connected the two homes. She certainly could not leave him home alone anymore. Who knows what he'd get into? And after the telephone call, there'd be a lovely visit with Maria, respite for Giovanna while Big Antonio, Maria's husband, took Pastore di Capre into the other room to play cards.

Big Antonio was shrinking with age. It seemed to him, he'd lost a centimeter or two in height and gained them around his waist. But he'd always be *Big* Antonio because his son was *Little* Antonio, a fifty-something-year-old balding fisherman, and his grandson, Antonio the third, was known only as Junior, a budding twenty-something-year-old at a military academy on the mainland. So, it was Big Antonio who played cards with Pastore, though it wasn't really a card game at this point. It was more like shuffling or dealing, any automatic action that gave Pastore di Capre the pleasure of familiarity where friends and family were slowly slipping into the unfamiliar.

Giovanna couldn't risk losing those visits. It was all she had left. So the telephone cord was yet again pulled from the wall, severing its connection and lying on the floor as useless as a stone.

From the harbor, Maria and Big Antonio's house looked as if it were the second floor of Giovanna's house. The grey stones and wooden shutters were exactly the same. The salty air and unrelenting southern winds wore them to the same degree, as with the other small stone homes along the ridge—most of them abandoned now. But Maria and Big Antonio's house was a second home to Giovanna and her husband, Pietro.

The villagers called him *Pastore di Capre*, meaning goat herder, even though his given name, like his father and grandfather, was Pietro. He and Carlo had been the only herders on the island. Others had a goat or two in their yards, but it was *Pietro*—Pastore di Capre—and Carlo who introduced those goats to the island and it was they who had the herd and the males for breeding, all of them climbing the peak to the pasture in the summer months.

The tavern owner's name was also Pietro, as was his father and grandfather for it was an island tradition hard to discourage— naming ones first son after oneself. So it might have become a bit confusing had they not all acquired nicknames that just seemed to present themselves at one time or another and then lay permanently like the stones embedded in the garden soil. For the tavern owner it was his two spindly chair legs that hung down from the short pant he'd worn as a boy that earned him the name *Chair*.

"Pietro come here," someone would call out, but he and several other boys would appear.

"No, not you," the person would shoo the others away as a finger would wag in his direction, "*Chair* legs here."

And then it was just *Chair*. The timeline was not straight in anyone's memory. The years went by, and *Chair* cemented itself in place. The tavern owner's name was Chair; that's all anyone knew.

There were also a few fishermen with the name Pietro, none of them known by their given name, each with his own acquired new-name that was old enough so that most could not even remember its origin. Thus if someone happened to come to the island looking for Pietro—after the war—there'd be no such person with that name. But if that person were asking for fresh goat milk or meat, well, then everyone knew Pastore di Capre and his friend Carlo were the men to see.

In the days after the war, the two young men would meet at the church before dawn and follow the goats up to the pasture, below an old castle whose broken walls remained from a time when Incompresso had made a worthy outpost for kings. The castle was a perfect place for the men to sit and watch the specks of boats in the distance or the thin line of that far off Mother Italia—a place where Carlo had been born and where the two men had fought side by side during the second Great War, far to the north at the Franco-Italian border. That was in the old days, of course, now the herd was gone. Carlo was gone. And Pastore di Capre was slowly disappearing.

But suddenly—so many years later, with Angelina far from home and Pastore di Capre but a whisper of his former self—Carlo had returned from the dead.

Giovanna had all but forgotten him, but there he was between her and her husband as they sat in the yard under the grape arbor near the gate and watched the boats in the harbor as evening blew in off the mountain. Big Antonio had come from the side of the house and was struggling to get the front gate open. Giovanna had wrapped a piece of wire around it to prevent Pastore di Capre from wandering away.

"Go help *Carlo*." Pastore di Capre was addressing Giovanna as he nodded his head at Big Antonio by the gate.

Giovanna and Big Antonio exchanged a look. They hadn't heard Pastore di Capre's voice so strong and clear in quite a few days.

"It's me, Pastore. Your neighbor." Big Antonio ignored Giovanna's reddened eyes as he tried to correct her husband. He worked the wire loose and opened the gate.

"I'm your neighbor. I'm Big Antonio." He pointed toward the roof above where his house lay and repeated, "your neighbor."

Pastore di Capre nodded his head. A breeze pushed past and a wisp of white hair fell across his face. It was difficult to cut his hair these days. He used to sit in the yard with a towel around his shoulders and Giovanna would carefully cut it with a pair of scissors that had no business cutting hair. But it was difficult to get him to sit for such a task anymore and what was the point? These days, Giovanna just put a comb in his hand each morning and his hand, remembering the automatic movement of a life-long ritual, carefully parted and combed and smoothed the hair down. That was good enough—until he walked outside into the sea breeze. And then the hair would blow straight up landing whichever way it wanted, giving him the appearance of a mad man.

Pastore di Capre looked at Big Antonio and put his finger to his mouth.

"Shh, Carlo. Giovanna is here."

He glanced sideways without moving his head. It was very childlike and Giovanna put her hand to her mouth and smiled.

Big Antonio looked at Giovanna, "Your daughter is on the phone from America. Go up. I'll sit here with him."

Giovanna was already half way out of the gate.

"Did she say she's coming back?" She asked. The pitch in her voice betrayed her calm demeanor as she tried to rewrap the wire on the gate.

"Leave it. Don't worry. He's not going anywhere."

She let out a sigh, wiped her hands on the front of her dress and trotted past them on the other side of the stone wall.

"Take your time," Big Antonio called as she disappeared behind the house. "Pastore and I—we'll have a nice visit, won't we, dear friend?" Big Antonio patted Pastore di Capre on the knee.

"Good thinking," Pastore di Capre whispered. "We'll talk about the gold."

"Yes," Big Antonio smiled. "The goats. They're fine."

Big Antonio's hearing was not what it used to be and he prided himself on his ability to placate Pastore di Capre, especially in the evenings when he seemed to get more agitated than ever. Whenever Pastore di Capre went into one of his rages—which seemed more often lately, if Big Antonio didn't hear it himself, he heard Giovanna calling to him from the back window and he'd be down in no time flat, an agile man for an eighty-five-year-old.

"You've got to, Carlo. Listen. We can't *leave* it there." His voice was barely audible. It took too much strength to push the words out.

"Yes, okay. I won't leave it." Big Antonio played along.

"It's bad, Carlo. Think of the gypsy."

"Yes. Yes. Okay." Big Antonio smiled and added, "I'm Antonio, though, Pastore. Antonio—Big Antonio."

"Antonio?"

"Yes."

Pastore di Capre was quiet for a few minutes. Big Antonio bent down and plucked a weed from the dirt. He sat looking at it, then began peeling the leaves off and throwing them down, watching them fall from his knees to his feet. The garden was in disarray. He remembered how Giovanna used to be meticulous with the rose bushes and those perfect rows of zinnias. He was trying to recall the name of the other flowers she used to plant when Pastore di Capre spoke again.

"The gold, Carlo."

"Okay," Big Antonio said quietly and this time he heard the word *gold* and his back stiffened against the chair. He looked up and noticed the weeds growing from between the stones in the garden wall and then his eyes went back to the dried zinnia stalks and the small mound of hard dirt behind them. He swallowed hard and looked at Pastore di Capre.

"No gold, Pastore. You mean goats."

"Goats?" Pastore di Capre scratched his head. He looked at Big Antonio with a furrowed brow that slowly ironed itself out to a straight line. He squinted his eyes and hissed, "You! Stay away from my wife." His teeth clenched tightly shut at the last word.

Big Antonio was somewhat taken aback. His head snapped up and he looked sideways at Pastore di Capre. He was about to say, "I'm helping Giovanna—nothing else." In fact, he got the first three words out before the blow to his face knocked him off the chair and left him sprawled out on the dirt.

The tavern owner, Chair, was on his way home for his evening meal. He left his grandson in charge most of the time.

"Whoa!" He pushed through the gate and grabbed Pastore di

Capre who was just half way between sitting and standing. "Sit down, Pastore."

Pastore di Capre squinted at Chair. "How about a drink?" he said with a quiet even tone.

"Come by the tavern sometime," Chair answered quickly.

"That's a good idea. I will," said Pastore di Capre and he sat down. It was the same exchange each time they saw one another. It started about a year or so before, but Chair wasn't sure exactly. He'd tried a few other friendly exchanges since, but none had produced a response from Pastore di Capre. Simply, whenever Pastore di Capre met Chair's eyes as he passed by in the evening, he'd say the same phrase, which Chair would follow with his response and Pastore di Capre seemed satisfied.

Chair knelt to help Big Antonio to a sitting position. The blood from his nose had spattered down the front of his shirt and was rushing from both nostrils.

Big Antonio was grunting and sputtering but couldn't quite get any words out. The images along the stone wall were blurry. He tried to focus on one of Chair's several faces that were spinning before him.

"Hold here," Chair said, putting Big Antonio's fingers to the bridge of his nose but Big Antonio's hand was limp. Chair exhales and whispered, "God Almighty."

By then, a few other passersby were in the yard ready to aid Chair.

"What happened?" Anna Maria, Giovanna's friend from church, was passing by and noticed the onlookers.

Pastore di Capre heard the question and attempted to answer. "Fight—boys fighting." It was barely a whisper. He clicked his tongue and shook his head in disapproval.

"Where's Giovanna?" she asked.

"With the baby," Pastore di Capre said. But it wasn't what he'd sent down from his brain. He'd wanted to say something different but somehow those were the words that seemed to be attached to the question of "Where's Giovanna?" It frustrated him. He tried again but all that came was the word "baby." So he stamped his foot in anger and balled his hands into fists.

"Grab a towel or something from inside the house." Chair motioned to Anna Maria with one hand. "Wet it—maybe some paper towels." And to Pastore di Capre he said, "Stop it, Pastore. Sit down!"

"How 'bout a drink."

"Come by the tavern sometime."

"That's a good idea. I will."

Big Antonio rolled his eyes.

Chair addressed Big Antonio, "Do you want to go to the medical center?"

He shook his head.

Anna Maria's daughter, Anna, was looking over the wall into the yard, her pregnant belly pushed against the stone where several other people craned to see what was happening.

"Anna, come and help," her mother yelled to her as she disappeared into the house. Moments later her voice rang from the open window. "Don't just stand there. Come and bring Pastore di Capre into the house before he gets into something else."

One of the observers at the wall quickly made her way to the side of the house and up the path to find Giovanna as Anna fumbled with the gate and waddled into the yard. She stood in front of Pastore di Capre and grabbed both his hands.

"Let's go into the house," she smiled. "It's getting too cool out here."

"Angelina." Pastore di Capre beamed, his eyes moist as he took Anna's hands.

"Anna." Anna said, correcting him.

"Anna?"

"Yes, Anna. Angelina is in America."

"Yes," Pastore di Capre stood slowly and Anna put her arm

around his shoulder as she guided him to the front door, just as her mother emerged with paper towels dripping with water in one hand held high and a striped dishtowel in the other hand.

"Keep him calm until Giovanna gets here."

Anna led him to the sofa and went to turn on the television.

"Oh no, no, no." Pastore di Capre lamented.

"No television?" Anna wasn't sure.

"No. No." Pastore di Capre shook his head several times and repeated the word. "No. No." He put his head in his hands and a muffled, "no" escaped.

Anna sat next to him, "Sh. It's okay. No T.V. Don't worry."

It seemed a bit dramatic for not wanting television, but Anna was at a loss. She rubbed his shoulder.

"Okay. Okay." She looked around the room and saw the silver lines of cobwebs on the photos near the window, alit by the setting sun. Nonna Giovanna had always been a meticulous housekeeper but it had been a while since Anna had been inside the house. When she was a little girl, the smell of baking as she passed the open gate used to prompt her to come inside and ask Giovanna if she wanted any help in the garden. She'd be rewarded with a piece of whatever it was coming out of the oven. She smiled and put her hand on her swollen belly.

"Nonna Giovanna is such a good cook, isn't she?"

Pastore di Capre looked up, nodded his head in agreement and said, "No—uh, oh—um." His voice petered out and he heaved a heavy sigh. Anna decided to proceed without him. She preferred her own voice to the silence of the house and muffled chaos of the yard.

"My baby," she put her hand on her belly, "is coming soon. I saw her on a sonogram at the medical center. She's perfect."

Pastore di Capre smiled, nodded and opened his mouth to say something but Anna continued, "You see this medal?" Her fingers pulled a tiny pendant of the Virgin Mary on a gold chain from inside her shirt. "My mother gave it to me when I told her I was pregnant. Her mother gave it to her."

Pastore di Capre reached up and touched the pendant. He seemed content, finally. Anna's voice soothed him.

"Someday, I will give it to my daughter. It guarantees a healthy baby, you know . . . and it's nice to have something to pass down, don't you think?" Anna didn't wait for an answer. "It's like the past continues into the present, right? It's kind of nice. A medal of Mary — solid gold, you know."

"Gold?" Pastore di Capre's head snapped up. "We have to go!" He was agitated, breathing hard through his nose and looking from side to side as he leaned forward and tried to get up but Anna had one hand on his shoulder and the other on his knee.

"Oh, Nonno Pastore, don't get up." The pressure of her hand pinned his leg to the sofa.

Pastore di Capre recognized a familiar voice from behind — a bit distant, perhaps in the front yard. "Giovanna?" his voice was raspy and had lost its power.

Giovanna came into the living room and snapped on the light. The dimly lit room brightened. Chair and Big Antonio followed her into the room. Maria had run behind her down the path, but with shorter legs and a stouter torso, she was just pushing through the doorway completely out of breath, and coming to the side of Big Antonio who had two large wads of paper protruding from each nostril.

"Oh my," she said. "Should we go to the medical center?"

He shook his head and said to Giovanna in a very nastily voice, "You sure you're okay?"

"Go take care of yourself, Antonio." Her eyes were wet and her face flushed. "I'm okay now." She looked at Maria and Maria put her hand on Giovanna's shoulder.

"Listen—" Maria hesitated. "Angelina will be back soon. Pasquale is not made to stay in America."

Anna got up with some effort and turned to see Giovanna wiping the back of her hand across her nose.

"Nonna Giovanna." She was at her side, putting her arms around the older woman—as best she could with the protrusion between them. "You need help with Nonno Pastore." She lowered her voice. "I didn't realize it was so bad. I'll come by more often."

Giovanna kissed the young woman on both cheeks. "Look at you. You're absolutely radiant." She smiled and continued, "ah yes, Anna, time certainly catches us off guard, doesn't it?" She laughed. It was small and weak, but it was genuine. "I'd love to see more of you."

Big Antonio let out a hearty laugh and almost shot the paper nose-plugs across the room. He put his hand to his nose as he said, "oh you'll see more of her alright!" and then he puffed out his cheeks and brought his arms around his torso imitating the round size of Anna's belly.

All four chuckled quietly and Pastore di Capre turned his body around on the sofa to see them. He had a big smile from ear to ear.

"He seems calmer now," Anna said.

"It's the sun, I think," Giovanna answered. "When it begins to lose its light, he gets very anxious. I'm not sure why. But the sun is gone now. He'll be okay."

"Then I'll come by tomorrow before sunset," Anna said.

Her mother entered the living area, from the yard. She held blood soaked paper towels and a striped dishtowel that had splotches of maroon. "That's not a bad idea," she said to her daughter as she brushed past on her way to the kitchen trash.

"Good evening, Pastore," she called as she reached the kitchen doorway.

Pastore di Capre repeated what he heard. "Good evening, Pastore," he said, then shook his head and sighed a heavy sigh of defeat.

Giovanna came to the back of the sofa and put her arms around Pastore di Capre. "It's okay, my love." She kissed his cheek lightly and said, "good evening, Anna Maria."

Pastore di Capre tried to imitate her but only repeated, *Maria,* which seemed to satisfy him though Anna Maria had already vanished into the kitchen.

"I'll see you tomorrow," young Anna said and Chair added, "maybe me too."

"Do you want me to stay awhile?" Maria, Big Antonio's wife, asked.

Giovanna turned and shook her head, then looked at Big Antonio.

"Do you think you can push the bed to the wall. It's too heavy for me. He's up and down a hundred times a night. I'm afraid I won't hear him."

She planned to sleep on the outside edge of the bed so as to feel Pastore di Capre if he tried to get up over her. Lately she was dead tired and knew she could no longer rely on just hearing him move about.

"Sure. Okay. Maria . . . come with me." He was still a little spooked by Pastore di Capre's accusation in the garden.

"You don't need my help," Maria answered.

"Just come."

Giovanna watched them retreat to the bedroom and then she heard water splashing in the kitchen sink and dishes clinking together and Anna Maria begin to hum.

Pastore di Capre closed his eyes and leaned his head back on the sofa. His thoughts were jumbled between time and space. He felt Carlo beside him—alive and well. They were two young men on the Franco-Italian border. Pastore di Capre's frostbitten feet forever reminding him of those days.

Both he and Carlo were among the poorest soldiers, village men without any connection to those who were creating the battle plans, but they also had grown up in the rough terrain that is fodder for making certain soldiers survivors. It was Carlo on the front line in the northern Alps who Pastore di Capre came to trust. The missions they were sent on were not supposed to be something they'd return from, but they did. Ragged and half starved, their only desires were for home when they'd finally made the decision to leave their posts.

For Pastore di Capre it was the peak above his island he longed for and for Carlo his beloved village on the mainland in Italy's southern arch. After a two-month trek, they'd finally rested in Carlo's village, a rest that was supposed to bring peace and renewal. But Carlo's parents had been buried in the graveyard only days before his return. His older brother lay beside them—another casualty of war and his sisters bickered among themselves for the goats that remained after most had been confiscated by the town's self-appointed mayor, as payment for imaginary services against which they were unable to defend themselves. They did what they could to protect the few remaining goats from hungry wolves and hungry villagers. It was just another scene of the war. The sisters were ragged and wild-eyed. They'd been born into poverty and war, and knew nothing else. It pained Carlo to see them so, but not a pain as deep as his own. Yes, the terrain made soldiers who survived but the war made soldiers with hearts of stone.

"We will care for the goats. Rest, dear sisters." Carlo reassured them as he prepared to do the unthinkable.

He could have lived there in the mainland's southern mountains indefinitely and no one would have been the wiser. The peasants of the south felt no allegiance to their brethren in the north and with each gravesite dug, with each new broken body returned home, their lack of allegiance cemented into defiance so it would have been easy for Carlo to stay in his village, protect his sisters and live a quiet though meager life. But the sacrifices he'd made—the young years he'd given to his country, the sins he'd committed against humanity—had turned him into a selfish man. And Pastore di Capre did not try to discourage him. They left one female goat and then took the other five goats and walked toward the coast, their pockets bulging with the gold coins that had been hidden in the well.

"How will the goats survive on Incompresso?" Pastore di Capre did not know anything about goats. "There is very little greenery—only a small pasture, high up above the sea. Quite a climb it is, too."

Carlo pressed his lips together and tried to smile, but his smile was left behind in the courtyard of his village. An island—one he'd never laid eyes on—seemed the perfect escape from a world in which he no longer wished to be a part.

"Goats have a resilience and an ability to survive under the worst conditions. Don't worry. We have the male. We'll have a small herd by next year."

It wasn't unusual to see animals on the ferry. Sometimes, there'd be a stray cat or two that the captain allowed—sometimes a passenger with a few live chickens. But in ordinary times, five goats would have brought admonishment from the ferry captain and perhaps an inconvenient departure delay caused by a long drawn out negotiation. Those were hungry years, though, so a quick gift of a female goat for the captain, who'd had his fill of fish and whose wife was on board that day, ensured safe passage without questions.

The island welcomed its returning son and accepted the newcomer with his animals. The men were happy to find a place to rest. They climbed to the upper pasture with their goats to laze under the cool lip of the cave far above the village near the broken castle.

Each day, they'd watch the small dots of fishing boats as they left harbor in the silver light of dawn and when the sun was too hot, Pastore di Capre and Carlo would follow the goats to the cave opening and lie in the shade until evening when they'd secure the goats inside the goat shed. Then they'd descend the mountain like upright oxen with full milk cans hanging from either side of a long tree branch perched behind their necks. They became known as the two goat herders—*due Pastori di Capre*—in the island dialect—and the name Pietro, Pastore di Capre's given name, slowly made its departure.

The tavern was often the place they'd stop to have a drink with a few fishermen before returning home to a meal Pastore di Capre's mother had prepared.

One son had left to fight in Italy's war and two had returned. The Saint Antonio medal she put around her son's neck was meant to keep his return to the island a permanent one. Her dear friend had sent her son, Antonio, to give it to her. He had also returned safely from the war and had brought with him two Saint Antonio medallions. They were unusual in that the saint stood atop a tiny sparkling stone—a diamond, the jeweler had told him—though Antonio had serious doubts. But it was so unlike any medallion he'd ever seen, so he'd bought one for himself and one for his mother. She'd attached it to a sturdy chain and had insisted in giving it to her dear friend's son, Pietro—Pastore di Capre. But first Antonio had inscribe two horns on the back of the medal just as he'd done to his own, to ward off *malocchio*, the evil eye, for superstition lay upon religion like a whore in a brothel.

With pride, Antonio showed the inscription to Pastore di Capre's mother before she presented it to her son. But it was that inscription, years later that would haunt Antonio as he married and created his own little Antonio—transforming himself into *Big Antonio*.

Pastore di Capre's mother was overcome with gratitude at her son's return. She simply placed the medal around his neck and whispered a prayer. She did not argue with her son when she noticed its absence several days later. She trusted his judgment. Nor did she argue when he refused to speak to Carlo about marrying his sister. After all, if he felt this man to whom he seemed to rely above everyone else was not fit to marry his sister, well then, she had to bow to his decision—for no one on the island knew Carlo as well as he.

So, although Carlo's sudden and bizarre death was quite upsetting, Pastore di Capre's explanation of the mishap satisfied the villagers when he came down to get help in removing Carlo's body from the narrow crevice inside the cave. It happened only days after Pastore di Capre's wife, Giovanna, lost another child so the villagers were sensitive to hers and Pastore di Capre's grief with the stillborn death of their son. They were all so absorbed with the sorrow that hung like a fog above the island, that the death of a stranger was barely a blip on a radar screen—it mattered not at all that Carlo had been a resident among them for two years. But for Pastore di Capre, it was the day he began his slow decent into darkness.

With thoughts of Carlo jumbled in his head, Pastore Di Capre leaned his head back on the sofa and drifted off to a restless sleep. Giovanna sat beside him and rested her head on his shoulder. She thought of Angelina and the conversation they'd had moments before on Maria's telephone and she closed her eyes and followed her Pietro into a light slumber.

CHAPTER 5

Angelina stood in the tiny apartment looking out the window over the hot plate. She saw Gina's roof through the dark shadows of tree branches against the night sky and she imagined Gina's husband lying on the sofa, the same sofa she'd seen while Gina was bandaging her elbow.

She thought of her son, Rocco. How could a mother nurse an infant at her breast, protect him with the instinct of a she wolf, nurture each growing moment, only to watch him emerge as an adolescent—and have so much of it go wrong? He was just a child, only a small boy when he was sent away. But what could have been done to change it? Murder—he took away someone else's son, a life sentence for that mother. Murderers have to be punished, but weren't they bad boys that came from bad mothers? Her Rocco was such a sweet sensitive child—so warm and loving. It hadn't made sense then. It didn't make sense now.

The sound of muffled footsteps clopping up the hallway stairs caught her attention. The shuffling feet hesitated outside the door before Pasquale opened it and entered.

Angelina craned her neck to see behind him.

"Where're the children?"

"They went out together. They need a bit of fun, no?" He closed the door. "I let them take the car. They'll be fine."

"Together? Did they say where?"

"Something about ice cream, I think. It's okay. Don't worry."

"Pasquale."

"They're two adults. And they know the language. They'll be fine."

"Pasquale." It was the way she said his name — *Pasquale* instead of Pat — he knew what it meant.

"Rocco will be fine." Pasquale tried to avoid the unpleasant conversation ahead. "There are plenty like him here. Look at Javier. He's married, has children and still no papers. It's okay."

After Pasquale had bought the store from his cousin, it was Javier who had taught him the correct way to throw the pizza dough. He'd come with the store, like the appliances and fixtures and he had expected that he'd be there always but lately Javier had been pestering Pasquale to make him a partner. It was obvious that Rocco was not at all the man his father was and Javier had invested half his adult life in that pizzeria. He didn't want to rely on Rocco for his future.

"I don't think it's fine. You shouldn't have let them go," Angelina said. "He has to be legitimate or his past will destroy his present." She bent and picked up a bottle of clear liquid that sat beside the refrigerator. "What if the police stop the car for some reason?"

"That won't happen. They're just going down the street for ice cream. Completely innocent. There'd be no reason for such a thing."

Pasquale had his eye on the bottle of grappa in Angelina's hand. "Ah, good idea," he said, "pour me a glass. I'll go take a quick shower."

Angelina had brought the grappa from home on this past visit. Her mother had wrapped several articles of clothing around it while she'd helped her pack.

"This will warm you when America gets too cold," Giovanna had said to her daughter, but she'd been thinking, "*Don't forget me here. See this bottle in your American home, and remember me. Remember I'm waiting."*

And actually, Giovanna's strategy worked, for Angelina stood staring at the bottle now, listening to the shower water splash behind the closed door, weighed down by guilt from the memory of watching her mother grow smaller and smaller, as Angelina stood on the ferry moving away from the island. She sighed and poured two small glasses.

A few minutes later, Pasquale emerged from the bathroom with a towel wrapped around his waist and Angelina lay half asleep on the sofa, her glass of grappa, almost empty.

"You started without me." He sat on the sofa.

"Pat, let's bring them here," Angelina's eyelids were heavy and her lips slow and labored with the words.

"What? Who?"

"My parents." Angelina sat upright and handed Pasquale his glass. "We can get better care for my father here. I can see them every day. We can be together."

"Here? In this apartment? It's too small."

"We have enough to get a bigger apartment. Maybe we can buy a house like the ones behind us." She nodded her head to the window above the hotplate. "Please, Pat. Let's consider it."

Pasquale took a sip and put his glass on the table. He didn't want to consider it. He didn't want his in-laws here. He was carefully weighing his words, formulating something that would not create a battle between them when Angelina slid over the sofa cushion and put her arm around his neck, gently kissing his cheek. He turned and kissed her on the mouth and remembered the ironworks bench as her hand slid into the opening of the towel, stirring his youth. A soldier standing at full attention, ready for command.

*   *   *   *

Patrice had the car's overhead light on and was reading the address on a newspaper advertisement whose edges were creased from folding and unfolding so much that it was like a limp lettuce leaf in her hand. She looked at the map on her phone.

"Make a right here."

"Here?"

"Wait, no. I lost the signal. At the next corner, I think."

"It's getting late Patrice. We've got to get up early."

"Just one drink. Hey—there it is, over there. You see the orange sign?"

Rocco pulled into a parking lot. "There aren't that many cars," he said, "on a Saturday night? What kind of place is this?"

Patrice did not answer. Her hand was on the door waiting for the car to stop. Her feet hit the blacktop just as the engine cut and she was way ahead of Rocco—almost skipping—by the time he got out of the car and trotted after her. They approached the entrance together and heard the bass pounding through the open door. An oversized guy with arms like a gorilla stopped them.

"I.D.?"

"Huh?" It sounded to Patrice like "I did" and though both she and Rocco had a good command of English, her nervousness was getting the better of her. Rocco understood and was about to ask a question, when a smaller guy emerged from behind the gorilla-man and said, "It's okay, Matt. She's with me."

Rocco was ready to flatten him against the building as the guy reached his hand out to Patrice but Patrice managed to say, "Hi Josh," through a high pitched giggle that knocked the breath from Rocco. She reached her hand out to meet his.

"Wait a minute." Rocco said it loud and slowly with a punch between each word. "Patrice? No way. This is not happening." His blood was flowing into his two tight fists as the gorilla-man stood between him and Patrice who was being pulled toward Josh by Josh's grip.

"Rocco it's okay," she said.

"Yeah, Rocco," said the gorilla-man with a smile, "Looks like she's done with you. Your girlfriend's dumping you, don't you think?" He had his hand on Rocco's chest.

"He's my brother," Patrice said.

"Oooh." Gorilla-man's hand shot down to his side. He looked at Josh, "Hey, what are you doing?"

"It's okay," Patrice said to all three of them, "Really."

"Listen," Gorilla-man said. He was looking at Rocco but the message was for all of them, "you can come in but no trouble. Got it?"

Rocco thought back to the island. He thought of his first time in a club — which also happened to be his last — when he and friends took the afternoon ferry to the mainland. And the jail sentence that followed in its wake. He composed himself, said nothing and nodded his head.

How did Patrice know this guy?

The three walked into the dark entrance. Rocco watched the black orbs of Patrice's and Josh's heads silhouetted against the colored strobes in front of them as the entrance opened into a large not-too-crowded bar. Their heads were pressed together and Josh was yelling into Patrice's ear so as to be heard over the music coming from a band on a small platform.

"I wouldn't have been able to get the car," she yelled back at him. "I can't drive. And I doubt my father would have let me come alone."

Rocco heard the last few words. He grabbed Patrice's arm.

"Who is this guy? How do you know him?"

Patrice pulled from his grasp and shook her head. She yelled over the noise. "He's a friend. We met online." She stepped back and was holding Josh's shoulder, ready to introduce him as if they were simple friends from school, back on the island, but Rocco moved in closer to Patrice and ignored Josh.

"You have an hour. One hour." He held one finger up for emphasis. "And no drinking. And don't go too far. I don't want to look for you. One hour. Meet me at the car if we get separated."

But Rocco had no intention of getting separated, though he was somewhat captivated by the lights and music. And he really hadn't had much fun since he'd gotten out of jail so he was somewhat intrigued by the American club. As he watched Josh and Patrice move toward the band, he suddenly noticed three scantily clad young girls, eyeing him from the far side of the bar. They had their heads bent inward and were talking rapidly and then they all turned toward him and smiled. He made his way to the bar, a few feet from them.

Now, what should he order—he didn't know what existed, really. He'd occasionally have a few beers after work while watching television in the apartment above the pizzeria. Maybe he should order a beer. It's not that he was terribly ignorant—not at all. Inexperienced would be a more accurate description. He just didn't know what people in bars ordered, except for those on television. It was common for children on Incompresso to have wine with dinner, a small cup with a few sips mixed with water. But wine was not something a person would order in this type of place and he knew that.

There was a gaping hole in his repertoire of experiences. He knew that too. He simply hadn't had much time to experiment with Adolescence's little playbook before he'd been locked away from the rapidly changing world. Those chances to test the waters of authority had disappeared the day he was sent to jail. Well, it wasn't really jail, actually. He was only fifteen at the time, so he'd been sent to the work camp for wayward boys on the mainland. He spent a few hours in the morning in a small damp room, crowded together with other boys, some as young as ten, listening to a so-called-teacher drone on, in what was supposed to be the mandatory education of a juvenile offender. That was followed by hours of hard labor as the boys were farmed out—under the radar, away from the protective eyes of state reformers—as free laborers to the locals. The only positive aspect, as Rocco saw it, was that he'd learned to drive a tractor and a pickup truck while working on one of the farms. At one point, some older boys taught him how to roll a truck down an incline while in second gear, press the clutch and get the engine running — no key necessary — or permission of the owner.

So the residents of Incompresso knew that young Rocco was spending his adolescent years in *jail* and maybe it would do him some good, for he was a bit of a live wire, some said. Of course, none said that in earshot of his parents or his grandparents. And it mattered not at all that it was not actually jail, which is barely worth mentioning since eventually that's where he landed.

What else could be expected? Released at the age of twenty-one without an actual education, without a soul to meet him at the work camp gate, given the customary ten thousand lira, the equivalent of about ten dollars, and a pat on the back. He spent all the money on a train ticket to the port. He knew that the ferry captain would let him aboard — money or no money. How was he to know that the train was going to a different port? He'd never bought a train ticket before. He knew only what he remembered from the island and what he'd learned from the other boy's in the camp. So when he'd ended up on the western shin of Italy, penniless and aching to see his island, he used the only knowledge he'd gained during that six-year stint with the state. He stole a car with the intention of driving it to the correct port, which he might have been able to do if he'd only known the basics of direction and geography.

So at twenty-one years of age, having been locked away for six years, every movement dictated by the guards, never having experience the kiss of a woman or the buzz of a hard drink, he was sent back to jail. This time it was really jail. But his paternal grandfather, Old Rocco, dead in his grave, returned to help his grandson, his namesake. Without him, young Rocco might have spent the rest of his life behind bars. The judge was a sentimental old guy. He remembered his childhood. His father had been a journalist who'd spent time on Incompresso so the judge was more interested in talking to the boy about the sketches his father had left behind and about Old Rocco the fisherman.

"Yes," Rocco told him, "That was my grandfather — my father's father."

He told the judge all that he could remember but, after all, he'd never really met that grandfather as he was born the same day Old Rocco had died in the earthquake. Well, that was all the judge needed to hear for he was as superstitious as he was sentimental. And though the law would not allow him to free Rocco as he truly wished he could, it did allow him to give the minimum sentence for a returning offender. Four years. Rocco promised the old judge to play by the rules, get out as quickly as possible and return to the island. Yet now he was further from the island than he'd ever dreamed, and with no hope of return as he stood at a bar in an American club. His elbow sat on the shiny damp surface of the bar as the bartender waited.

The three young girls continued talking to each other and looking at him until one dressed in torn jeans and a very small, bikini-like top, gave a quick nod to her friends and sauntered toward Rocco, on a dare. She was holding an empty beer bottle.

Rocco looked at the bartender.

"I'll have a beer," he yelled over the music. The girl smiled at him. "Make it two," Rocco added.

She squeezed between an occupied barstool and Rocco as she put her empty bottle on the bar. The bartender brought the two beers over and placed the bottles on the bar. The girl nodded her head and said something to Rocco but the music was too loud so he bent his head down to her face and said, "What?"

The bartender was waiting. Rocco glanced at him and saw him holding both hands in the air with ten fingers extended. So Rocco reached into his back pocket to get his wallet as the girl brought her lips close to his ear and said, "What's your name?"

Her warm breath hit his ear canal and vibrated inward tickling the edges as it made it's way to the eardrum. He felt the sensation run down his neck and into his torso as he opened his wallet and realized he had only one ten dollar bill—the change from the fifty his father had given him for gas. He handed it to the bartender and replaced his wallet.

"Rocco," he answered the girl. "What's yours?"

Whatever her name was, escaped him and wafted up into the chaos of the music. She smiled and looked at the two beer bottles, one in each of his hands. Rocco looked down at them also and remembered they were there. He held one out to her and said, "beer?"

"Thanks." The band had stopped playing at that moment and her voice was loud—smacking against Rocco's face.

She took the beer and said, "gotta get back to my friends," who were watching intently. She had taken the dare and won the challenge. And Rocco watched her retreat with a sense of loss mixed with shame.

"*Idiot!*" he thought to himself and then scanned the crowd for Patrice but didn't see her.

Patrice was behind the building with Josh. There were a few chairs and tables set up on a makeshift patio. It wasn't part of the club but it was a place to come and rest from the music or smoke a cigarette. They were sitting side by side at one of the tables. Josh had been to the pizzeria a few times after Patrice had told him where it was and the last time had handed her the advertisement that sat crumpled in her front pocket.

"Really, next time I'll come alone," Patrice said.

"I can pick you up," Josh said as he lit a cigarette.

"Oh God, no. My father—he's not from here. He's kind of protective, especially since my brother went—uh well— sometimes he gets a little crazy with us. Even with my mother."

"Nothing wrong with that," Josh said as he blew the smoke out of his mouth and Patrice batted it away from her face.

"Oh sorry." Josh put his hand behind him and the smoke

floated away as the embers fell to the cement. "That's a good thing. Your father, I mean. Wish my father had been like that."

"He's not?"

"Not really." Josh paused. "No, definitely not. Haven't seen him since I was a little kid."

"He's away?"

"Divorced. When I was young."

Patrice looked down at the empty table.

"Oh." She wasn't sure what to say. He was the first person she'd met who had divorced parents. People on Incompresso never divorced. Marriage was forever whether you wanted it or not. Divorce was for characters on serial television or for movie stars.

"Well, who knows?" she said. "Things happen between people. You know—it's never the kid's fault." She remembered having read that somewhere.

"I love your accent," Josh said, "when I came to the restaurant and heard you talk, it was so great. It wasn't the same over the phone."

"Restaurant? Oh God, that's barely a store but it's definitely not a restaurant." Patrice laughed.

"Hey. It's something. It's not easy to make a business work these days, especially not in this area."

"What about the garage?"

"The what?" Josh leaned sideways off his chair and bent his head back as far away from Patrice as he could without falling over. He brought the cigarette to his mouth, inhaled and blew the smoke hard into a line of gray, behind him and away from Patrice.

"The picture on Facebook," Patrice said, "The garage? You know—the background picture—your profile with the cars?"

"Oh, yeah that. Well, it's actually part of a dealership. I work there, in the shop." He quickly added, "it's good money. Auto mechanic is a good job, but well—it's not like having a business. Like you."

"Business?" Patrice shook her head. "I have nothing, Josh. I'm pretty sure when I go back to Incompresso, I'll leave with whatever I came." She put her hand on his.

"You're ice cold." Josh looked down at her hand and added, "let's go sit in my car."

He threw the cigarette to the concrete patio and stepped on it. "You probably don't smoke weed either, right?"

"Weed?" She knew the word from gardening shows on television and her past English lessons, but didn't understand what he meant.

"Ya know—pot," Josh tried again.

Also a word she knew but still she didn't get it. The few slang words she'd heard on American television even had her mother guessing at meaning. But certainly neither had ever learned the slang for marijuana, though Patrice was no stranger to it.

Nonna Giovanna had watered it in her garden for one whole season when Patrice and her friend, Daniela, had planted it there—mostly just to see if they could. One of the crew on the ferry had introduced them to cannabis when they were in high school. It made them laugh so hard at nothing at all and was a welcome diversion from the mundane life of the island. When he was in port, the crewman stopped at the tavern for a few hours where Patrice and Daniela could find him. He always left them with the crumpled remains at the bottom of the bag, which they'd stuff into a homemade aluminum foil pipe when they found a private place to smoke it safely—usually in Nonna Giovanna's yard.

"What's that you're burning there, girls?" she'd ask. "Is that the incense again?"

A few times they collected the seeds that they found among the crushed leaves and planted them between Nonna Giovanna's zinnias. Patrice hadn't even noticed the seedling of one fortunate plant that made it past the zinnia buds until Nonna Giovanna casually mentioned it to her.

They were standing beside one another at the kitchen sink after a large evening meal. The rest of the family was in the yard, enjoying the sunset and the cool breeze from the harbor. Patrice almost dropped the serving dish she was drying. Her hand, wrapped in a striped dishtowel, was sweeping around the edges of the platter as Nonna Giovanna, her hands submerged in soapy water, matter-of-factly said to her, "Your purple flower finally made it."

Patrice's hand stopped mid-wipe. "Purple flower?"

"You know—the one you and Daniela keep planting. It's growing. I saw it this morning. Did you know it was going to be so tall? It's taller than my zinnias."

"No kidding?" Patrice suppressed a laugh and felt something like pride.

And so Nonna Giovanna tended to the marijuana plant, carefully weeding around it and watering it faithfully so as to protect her granddaughter's creation.

Until the tavern owner's grandson happened by one day and asked, "Geez, Nonna Giovanna, do you know what that is, that you're watering?"

So when Josh opened the glove compartment in his car and pulled out the plastic bag, Patrice laughed.

"Oh, cannabis," she said and cracked open the window a tiny bit. "What's this?" Patrice pulled a square silver packet the size of her palm from the bag. There was a metallic green drawing on the cover with menacing eyes drawn into it.

"Spice. K-2," Josh said and took the packet from her hand and threw it back into the glove compartment. "We could do that another time, if you want." He hesitated. "If you think we'll see each other again."

Patrice's smile pulled into her eyes but then suddenly fell flat. "Oh look," she pointed past Josh. "I think that's my brother. Come and talk to him. I need him on my side or this won't work."

Josh's heart banged against his ribs, "Where? Does he see *us*?"

"There," she said.

Josh's eyes followed her pointing arm.

She continued, "He's leaning on our car. That's where we said we'd meet if we got separated. It's okay. He's cool."

"Uh, it didn't really seem that way before."

"He's just annoyed that he didn't know about you. I wasn't sure he'd bring me. I couldn't risk it so I gave him some nonsense story about going for ice cream. He's just as crazy as I am with staying in that pizzeria all the time." Patrice put her hand on the door handle, "Believe me, he was perfectly happy to get out tonight. Come on."

She opened the door.

It was true. Rocco leaned against the car stewing over the fact that his sister had made a friend in America, someone who seemed genuinely glad to see her. They'd both been trapped within that small pizzeria, ascending and descending the stuffy stairs in the back hallway, day after day, and yet Patrice had actually found a way out. She'd left the pizzeria—who knows how many times—using her telephone and an *internet* connection. She was six years younger but eons ahead of him. He looked up at the sound of footsteps on the pavement and saw Patrice approaching. Josh was at a slower pace, a few steps behind. Patrice saw the little-boy-lost look on Rocco's face before he could harden his forehead and squint his eyes transforming his gaze to angry-older-brother. Josh saw only the latter and slowed his pace a bit more.

Patrice held out her arms and said, "An hour! We made it." She glanced back at Josh, "Right Josh?"

He laughed nervously, "Yeah."

"What do you mean *we*?" Rocco growled.

"Rocco, you know as well as I do, that we'll go back to the store and be stuck there for who knows how long."

"Hey, Josh?" a pair of young men were walking by, "How's it goin' man?"

Josh turned to greet two friends, "Good. How're you guys doing?"

Patrice felt Josh take a few steps away from her and quickly continued as she looked from the two newcomers to Josh and back to Rocco, "Let's have some fun?" It was a question.

"You're not with Ashley anymore?" one of the passersby was addressing Josh who shook his head in response and looked at Patrice and then back at the one who'd asked the question. And he took a few more steps away from Patrice, saying something that she could not quite make out as Rocco responded to her.

"Patrice, what are you talking about?"

She looked back at Rocco, "Let's just hang out a little while longer."

"Who's the old guy?" one of Josh's friends whispered.

Rocco heard it and instead of anger, he felt frustrated. It was great looking older when he was a kid but now it felt like it would exclude him from that which he wasn't even sure he wanted to be a part.

"Who're you calling an old guy?" Rocco said it with a laugh and Patrice exhaled a cloud of relief as her shoulders felt the tension dissipate. "I'm probably younger than you." He smiled. "Name's Rocco." He nodded his head in greeting.

"Sorry man—it's dark, you know?"

"No problem."

"Hey where're you from? Your accent."

"Italy."

"Huh, not what I expected." The young man turned to his friend. "This is Neftali. He's from—where're you from?"

"El Salvador," the other said and shook his head with a loud sigh.

"Oh yeah, don't have a hemorrhage." He pointed to his own chest. "Chris." Chris' eyes went toward Patrice. All three—Patrice, Rocco and Josh—made the introduction in unison as they said, "Patrice," and then laughed.

"You're not leaving, are you?" Chris asked.

"No, not yet," Rocco answered as he glanced at his sister and smiled.

"Just came out to smoke," Josh said as he fumbled in his jeans pocket and took out a crumpled pack of cigarettes. He offered the pack to Rocco, who took it.

"Thanks."

Patrice watched her brother light a cigarette with Josh's lighter and suck the smoke in. It immediately left through his nose and his eyes filled with water.

"We'll meet you in there," Neftali said as he tilted his head to the door of the bar. He and Chris walked away.

Rocco remembered his empty wallet.

Josh said, "they're good guys," as he watched his friends retreat.

"Uh, you know. I'm not sure we should go back in," Rocco said, "It's getting late."

"What?!" Patrice turned on her heels and looked at Rocco. "You just said —"

Rocco decided to come clean. "I have no money, Patrice. If you'd have told me where we were going, I'd be prepared. What do you expect?" He coughed. More smoke came from his nose.

She sighed.

Josh kicked the sand in a tiny pothole at his feet. He was trying to decide whether or not to offer to pay.

"Don't worry about it. It's on me." He practiced the line in his head and worried it might be too humiliating for Rocco. But what if Rocco was okay with it and drank all night. Josh didn't have that much money in his wallet or on his card.

"Listen," Josh said, "Drinks are ridiculous in there. I was actually going to smoke a little weed in my car, then go back in to listen to the band."

As the words escaped, he suddenly wondered how Rocco would take them.

"Weed?" Rocco looked at Patrice for help.

"Cannabis," she said slowly, watching her brother carefully. "Let's do it." She was nodding her head lightly, "come on." She gently elbowed her brother's side.

"Well, this is a new one," thought Rocco. Since he'd been home — or more accurately — not locked up, he'd been on a wild roller coaster ride, freefalling with one shock after another as he was reintroduced to a world that simply didn't exist when he'd gone away. He felt the chug-chug-chug of the roller coaster car as it made it's slow laborious climb with each new task he had to learn, sometimes a simple greeting or look, and then the stomach-churning, throat-closing dive down the track each time a new shocking revelation was made.

"So, Patrice smokes cannabis."

"Okay." Rocco's voice was small. Patrice looked at Josh with a big smile.

*   *   *   *

When Rocco and Patrice finally found their way home after several wrong turns as every corner in America seemed to look the same, especially in the dark and in their altered state, Rocco pulled next to the dumpster behind the store and opened the door of the car. He slid his legs to the asphalt and tilted his head up.

"Light's still on in the living room."

"Shh. quiet," Patrice said with a laugh as she came around the car, "you'll wake up your girlfriend." She nodded toward the trees behind them. Their voices seemed to echo off the branches, which were swaying against the blue-black sky to the rhythm of the distant highway's traffic. The highway was at least three or four miles away and yet Patrice was hearing its dull song for the first time, her head bent up still watching the branches.

"Girlfriend?" Rocco asked as he slammed the car door shut.

"Jane." Patrice looked at him, "I heard Mama and Papa talking.

She lives back there somewhere." She pointed to the trees.

"No kidding?" Rocco focused in on the gray outline of rooftops behind the trees. "Do you know which one?"

"Which one what?"

"Which house?"

"Those are houses? I thought that was an apartment building." Patrice looked closely at the shadows behind the tree branches.

"Look at the roof," she said moving her arm as if she were tracing a jagged line.

"No." Rocco said, "They're houses. There're spaces between them. See?"

They both stood looking at the rooflines for a several seconds. Neither said a word. Then Rocco turned and walked toward the back door of the store as Patrice continued to squint at the shadows.

Rocco fumbled with the key until it clicked its way in and the door pushed inward. "Come on." He motioned to Patrice with his hand. "Let's go."

Patrice followed him in.

"Feel like pizza?" Rocco asked, "I could fire up the ovens."

"Ugh." The door closed behind them and Patrice said, "Not only do I not want pizza right now, I don't want it tomorrow or the next day or the next . . . " Her voice trailed off and Rocco snorted a quiet chuckle as he turned to her.

"How about some of Nonna's biscuits?"

The two were standing in the small square foyer where a set of dully-lit stairs led to the apartment and a large metal door at their side led to the store. The square was strewn with an array of footwear — dirty sneakers, boots, sandals — and a broken umbrella that stood in a corner next to a bicycle pump and a greasy toolbox with a missing latch.

Patrice sucked in hard, her eyes widening in surprise "You? You know how to make the biscuits?" She didn't wait for an answer. "Oh," it was more of a whisper and accompanied a sigh with enough longing for them both. "With honey?"

Now the key was in the metal door to the store as Rocco braced his foot against the bottom and tried to turn it. *"We don't have any honey,"* he thought and then said, "We can make honey with sugar and water."

"Did you just call me honey, honey?" Patrice squeezed the last word out with a laugh that infected Rocco and the two stood there trying to laugh in a whisper which was really impossible and actually ended up amplifying the sound which turned out to be similar to that of fighting raccoons which is what Pasquale thought as he was roused from his sleep upstairs in the apartment.

The low volume at which Angelina had left the television when she disappeared into the bedroom leaving Pasquale on the sofa, blended with the raccoon noises. It took Pasquale a moment to remember where he was. And then he realized the raccoons were in the foyer downstairs and with the half-sleep that comes from being pulled from a deep glorious restful slumber, Pasquale failed to surmise how raccoons might have gotten into a locked door, only remembering their nocturnal raids of the dumpster before he'd gotten a proper lock for it. And he'd forgotten that Rocco and Patrice were not home.

In a matter of seconds, he stumbled to the corner and grabbed the broom, opened the cabinet under the hotplate and grabbed the lid to the spaghetti pot they used on rainy days for catching the drips. With one hand holding the broom out like a jousting knight and the other holding the lid up like a shield, he realized he had no free hand for the doorknob and dropped the lid with a monstrous clatter that had Angelina's bare feet sliding from the bed onto the wooden floor just as Pasquale opened the apartment door wide and grabbed his shield from the floor.

The vision of her father, both hands outstretched, one holding a broom and the other a spaghetti pot lid while the apartment light shone behind him creating a spiritual-like vision, brought Patrice to her knees with uncontrollable laughter. At the same time, Rocco twisted the car key in the store door with one more powerful yank, breaking it off so that a small round nub remained attached to the key chain.

"Oh," he said, nodding his head and then thought, *"That explains why it wouldn't open."* He turned and held up the key chain, the broken car-key nub still in his hand. He expected his father to see the humor in it as he had and as he thought Patrice had also, for now she was literally crouched on the floor, overcome with laughter. But when Rocco saw the knight at the top of the stairs he put his hand on Patrice's back and bent over with his own uncontrollable laughter. And then Angelina appeared behind Pasquale.

"Good Lord, are they drunk?"

Pasquale looked over his shoulder at his wife and did not answer.

"Ice cream?" Angelina shook her head and switched the foyer light on.

"Get up here, you two. Get some sleep. For God's sake, it's two in the morning—and it's Sunday!"

CHAPTER 6

Incompresso's Sunday church bells clanked their broken song in the distance. They never quite worked after the church was damaged by the earthquake and repaired by volunteers. Rather than the hearty clang-clang from the days before the bell tower had toppled, it was now more of a clang-dink that reminded the older generation of the destructive force of an unstable world. Cries from hungry sea gulls rang out between each bell toll, as the birds circled the docked fishing boats in the harbor, lamenting the empty nets.

Pastore di Capre sat on the chair that Giovanna had dragged from the kitchen to the hallway and placed outside the bathroom. She'd originally pushed the chair next to the bathroom washbasin because she knew she needed as little distance as possible from the water in the sink to Pastore di Capre's stubble on his chin. But then she wasn't able to navigate around the chair so she slid it into the hallway.

The shaving soap was sitting on the bathroom counter, the sink full of water, the razor poised and ready beside the shaving soap. Giovanna looked at Pastore di Capre's profile as he sat quietly in the chair, his hands in his lap. She should have done this before she'd helped him dress. If she dripped too much soap or water on the front of his shirt, he might catch cold. The desire to have him look presentable, to try once more to shave his six-day-old white stubble and have him back as the clean-shaven, well-dressed man she knew — might actually have him looking worse if she dropped water and soap on him and then had to abandon the project before it was finished.

Giovanna squeezed past the chair and went to the kitchen, grabbed a clean dishtowel and made her way back to Pastore di Capre in the hallway. She lifted his chin and began tucking the towel into the front of his shirt. It was something Pastore di Capre had done hundreds of times with a napkin so he felt the towel at his chin and gently pushed Giovanna's hands away. Then he continued tucking the edges of the towel into the front of his shirt but he was worried about the table — the dining table — it wasn't in front of him when he took his fingers from his neck and went to lay them on the table. His hands fell to his lap and he smoothed them along his pant legs from the thigh to the knee several times.

Giovanna stood for a moment and listened to the broken church bells ringing.

She took a deep breath and said quietly, "Let's get to it, then."

"Let's," Pastore di Capre smiled and met her eyes and he was there briefly, just long enough to give her hope.

Giovanna stood in the doorway of the bathroom and reached for the shaving soap. She poured some in her hand and brought it to Pastore di Capre's chin. Pastore di Capre opened his mouth like a baby bird waiting to be fed.

Giovanna put her other hand under his chin and pushed his mouth closed.

"Close your mouth, Pastore."

His teeth clinked together and his jaw became rigid. Then as Giovanna began to rub the soap onto his face, Pastore di Capre's jaw began to move up and down as if he were chewing.

"We're shaving, Pastore. Shaving." She reached into the bathroom and picked up the razor. She held it up for him to see. "Shaving. You see? Shaving." But her hand would not stay steady.

She felt small tremors running from her shoulder to her wrist and the razor felt as though it were made of iron.

Pastore di Capre stopped chewing and reached for the razor. Giovanna pulled it from his reach and tilted his head back by placing one finger under his chin and her thumb at the side.

"I'll do it. Just keep your head up."

Her voice prompted him to look at her and she wasn't able to get a wrinkle-free stretch of neck. She was afraid she'd cut him. Maybe he could still do it himself. She took his hand and opened it. When Pastore di Capre felt the razor handle he closed his fingers around it and opened his mouth.

"No!" Giovanna grabbed his wrist, "Close your mouth. You're shaving." She put one of her hands over his mouth and with the other began to navigate his hand with the razor to his cheek. But her hand was too weak. How was it that he was getting stronger and she weaker?

Pastore di Capre had never in his life shaved while sitting in a chair with a napkin tucked into his shirt. He was more confused than ever. He saw the narrow hallway walls and knew he neither ate nor shaved in such a place. He tasted the soap and knew it belonged in the bathroom and the hand that was at his lips was trying to silence him.

An enemy.

Giovanna felt the teeth open before she realized what was happening and then they clamped down on her little finger like a wolf with a goat. And the hand with the razor came up and slashed at her face.

The pitch and volume of her screams were sufficient for getting him to open his mouth, as well as to bring Maria running through the front door within seconds. She was dressed in her Sunday dress, a black scarf tied under her chin but when she saw Giovanna's eyebrow and the bridge of her nose, Maria quickly pulled the scarf off and held it to the side of Giovanna's bloody face.

"Antonio!" She called her husband's name several times and then noticed the razor in Pastore di Capre's hand.

In the medical center, Maria waited with Giovanna while someone ran to find the doctor. A nurse cleaned Giovanna's cuts with a brown substance and large square pieces of gauze. Each time Giovanna winced, Maria rubbed her shoulders and whispered comfort. She didn't know how to begin the conversation she wanted to have with Giovanna.

"I'll call Angelina for you, if you want," she said.

"What for? She can't come. What's the point? You'll only worry her."

"Gia, you cannot do—"

Giovanna put one hand up. "Not now, please. I can't. I just can't."

The nurse looked at Maria's dress, "You can go to church. Miss Giovanna might be a while. I think she needs stiches."

"No—I'll wait."

"Don't wait, Maria. Go. Go and light a candle for me, for Pastore. Go and ask God why?" Giovanna's voice faltered. "Go, please—for me."

Maria hesitated. "I'll come back afterwards. Stay here." Maria looked at the nurse. "Keep her here until I get back."

"She's not going anywhere." The nurse stepped on a pedal that opened the top of the trash and dropped the bloody gauze into it just as the doctor came into the examination room. It was a small room, as small as Giovanna's living room, barely a room for any kind of examination, so with the addition of the doctor, it seemed natural that Maria should leave.

"Okay. I'll see you in an hour."

"What have we here?" The young man said as Giovanna looked at the unfamiliar face and thought he might have been any one of the young people who came in the summer months to visit parents and grandparents. He couldn't have been more than sixteen or seventeen, she thought. He was wearing jeans, a very wrinkled tee shirt and tennis shoes without socks. Certainly a white coat or at the very least, socks, would have added to his age.

"Where's Doctor Michalina?" Giovanna asked as she pulled back from his hand that had rested on her shoulder, "She takes care of me."

"She's gone. Finished up last Wednesday. I'm Doctor Giovanni—call me Gianni." He smiled and held out his hand while the nurse pressed more gauze to Giovanna's eyebrow.

When Giovanna ignored his extended hand, the young man looked at some papers that lay on the nearby counter.

"Well, look at that," he said in a pitch he usually reserved for small children, "We have the same name—kind of."

Giovanna did not respond.

Normally, she would have heard about the change in doctors. There wasn't much more news around the island other than the occasional wedding or birth and the not-so-occasional funeral as she lost one friend after another. But the gossip surrounding the medical center doctors was the most common because the doctors were outsiders, none had ever stayed permanently and it seemed socially safe to squawk on about them. But she'd been so occupied lately. She rarely got out alone anymore. Taking Pastore di Capre out was like taking a toddler who kept her from finishing a full sentence or hearing the ongoing conversation. She'd have to ask Maria about this new doctor.

A little over an hour later, Maria returned as she had promised, though she was behind Father Marco who hobbled across the village square, half the church congregation trailing him. He was holding the stem of a gold challis with one hand, a red cloth folded and hanging from between two fingers, while his other hand lay on top of the challis, protecting the contents. His golden garments swept behind him, rustling with the movement of his legs.

The medical center would be too small to hold them all, this Father Marco knew, though he did not dislike the attention or the feel of the followers at his heels. When he arrived at the medical center door, he turned and nodded to Maria who reached for the door handle to open it. Then he looked at the small group behind him, closed his eyes briefly as he nodded his approval and quietly spoke.

"Bless all of you for your concern."

Those who had gathered felt the piety of their actions as his words hovered above them like an angel. Those passing by, in a brief moment of panic, wondered what holiday they'd forgotten and stepped closer to the group hoping it would seem as though they'd been there the entire time. Father Marco and Maria disappeared into the medical center as the small group slowly dispersed, some crossing themselves and kissing the rosary beads in their hands, some whispering a quick Hail Mary, and some with a perplexed expression and a few whispered questions.

Giovanna was delighted to see Father Marco. She was alone in the waiting room.

Father Marco spoke. "It's a hard road you walk, Giovanna."

He was only a few years older than she. In their early years he was a sought-after young man and Giovanna seemed to remember her parents mentioning him as a prospective husband, though it had probably been a conversation many other parents had had back then. Young Marco had the strength needed to survive the island and the intellect to solve the inevitable problems that arise in life. But he returned from the war with a commitment to a spiritual life and many conjectured that there must have been a bargain with God somewhere out on the battlefield. Now his familiar voice comforted her.

"We all have our cross to bear, Giovanna. The Lord, God Almighty—he places a burden upon us and it is not for us to know his reasons." Father Marco removed his hand from the top of the challis, placed the red cloth over his arm and put his hand out toward Giovanna.

"I've missed you in church," he said. "Stand and let me give you communion."

Giovanna's eyes sparkled with the tears that filled them. She began to stand before Father Marco and felt the warmth of his touch as he helped her to her feet.

"Giovanna, this is the body of Christ." Father Marco made the sign of the cross over the challis and then put his fingers into it and pulled out a wafer. Giovanna met his eyes briefly and then lowered her head in reverence. A small tear escaped from the corner of her eye and rolled toward Father Marco's fingers as he placed the communion on her outstretched tongue.

The wafer began to dissolve within her mouth and she swallowed hard closing her eyes to concentrate on its downward movement. It brought a comfort that embraced her as she made the sign of the cross and opened her eyes to Father Marco's gaze. Maria stood a few respectful paces behind him.

"We have several volunteers from the congregation," Father Marco began, "mostly women but a few men because, well—there are some things another woman should not do for your husband." Father Marco turned toward the door that led to the village square.

"Come." He put his hand on Giovanna's back. "Let us go and give Pastore di Capre his Sunday communion."

Maria opened the door and waited for the two to pass through before she followed. Father Marco continued. "There will be someone at your house every morning." Giovanna opened her mouth to protest as it seemed the correct way to respond to such attention—though it was exactly what she needed and the burden grew lighter as Father Marco put his hand up to stop her and continued to talk.

"Giovanna, you have been there to help your neighbors in need, now they are there to help you. If this were someone else who needed help, you would be among the first to volunteer. Am I right?" He barely waited for her to nod her head in agreement.

As they came to the garden wall and spied Big Antonio and

Pastore di Capre sitting on the same two chairs from the day prior, Father Marco waved his hand in a brief greeting accompanied with a smile and then turned quickly to Maria.

"Maria, if you find that Giovanna, here, is alone one morning, please come and see me. We must be sure someone comes every day."

"I'll take care of it, Father."

"Pastore! Antonio! Good morning to you," Father Marco waited for Giovanna to open the gate for him.

Pastore di Capre heard the familiar voice and saw the flowing garment make its way through the front gate. He stood up, a pronounced scowl upon his face. He lowered his head and waited.

Father Marco came and stood before him. He whispered a prayer, removed his hand from the top of the challis and stuck two fingers into it, bringing out another wafer.

Big Antonio, Giovanna and Maria each inhaled a hard gulp of air and held it as Father Marco brought his hand toward Pastore di Capre's open mouth and outstretched tongue.

"This is the body of Christ." The communion wafer went to the tongue, the tongue retreated behind the teeth and the mouth closed as Pastore di Capre, head down, brought his four fingers to his forehead, then his chest where his shirt was dotted with his wife's blood, and he crossed himself.

"Amen," he whispered as he sat and the three let out a collective sigh of relief.

Father Marco looked at Big Antonio.

"Uh." Big Antonio cleared his throat, "I ate breakfast, Father. I'm not—um, you know, uh ready."

Big Antonio hadn't been to church since the earthquake had destroyed it back in his younger days. He'd been part of the crew who'd helped rebuild it and was part of those responsible for the defective bell tower. With each stone that was cemented into place, his skepticism had been renewed. Returning from the war with others like Pastore di Capre, he'd needed the church to comfort him and show him he was back home even if it was filled with weeping widows and mothers. It was man's inhumanity against his brother that had produced the horrors he'd seen. He could accept that God did not have a hand in it. But when the harbor was flooded, devastation brought to his family and his friends, well—that was the end of God for him. But he liked Marco—they'd been friends in school and he'd understood the reason for taking up God's cloth. And he couldn't fault his wife for attending every Sunday. After all, the congregation was mostly women and it was a good way for her to visit with them, walking there and back.

"I see." Father Marco said to Big Antonio as he put the red cloth over the top of the challis. Of course, he knew that Big Antonio hadn't been inside the church in years but he thought he'd give it a try.

"Maybe next time." Father Marco cleared his throat and walked out the gate. As he rounded the corner on the other side of the wall, he called to them all, "God bless. I'll see you soon." And he lifted the challis in a departing wave.

Big Antonio looked at Maria, "I think I heard our telephone ringing about an hour ago." He cocked his head as if he might hear it at that moment. "I didn't want to leave Pastore."

"Maybe Angelina?" Maria asked, mostly to herself. She knew her own children would not use the telephone when they could easily walk across the courtyard and talk to her. She knew her grandson would not call from the academy at such an early hour on a Sunday morning. It had to be Angelina in America.

"Did you eat something?" Giovanna asked Big Antonio. She knew his breakfast comment to Father Marco was a lie. She didn't wait for an answer. She turned to Maria, "Angelina would never call at this time. It's early in the morning over there—maybe two or three in the morning. Even if the world were crumbling around her, she'd be sleeping."

She touched Pastore di Capre's shoulder, "come on." She was addressing them all, "Let's have something to eat. I have some caponata in the oven.

Pastore di Capre got to his feet and shuffled into the house beside her. Big Antonio brought him to the dining table in the small kitchen.

"You want me to change his shirt?"

"No. Leave it. He's quiet now," Maria answered, "why change?"

"She's right." Giovanna agreed as the two men took a seat beside each other.

Giovanna went to the oven and opened it while Maria reached above her and brought four bowls from the cabinet. Giovanna was bent, one hand on the oven door, the other on the countertop, ready to reach for the pan of food but she was frozen. She felt as if she'd fall if her hands were removed, as if her legs would not have the strength to keep her steady in that bent position.

"What? Giovanna, what's wrong?" Maria put the bowls on the countertop and bent to see into the oven window. "What is it?" She looked at the caponata inside and then at Giovanna, waiting for an explanation. But Giovanna's eyes were closed and her mouth open. She was a statue bent in front of the oven.

"I-I-I." Giovanna stuttered, "I'm not sure." She let out a sigh and grabbed the countertop with her other hand as the oven door clunked open and bounced on its hinges. Maria pulled the pan from the oven and closed the door.

Giovanna slowly began to straighten her body to a standing position.

"Good Lord, Giovanna. What's happening?" Maria was staring at her friend.

In the millisecond it took Giovanna to answer, a train of thoughts ran through Maria's mind—about Pastore di Capre—how he'd been strong and lucid only months before. About Angelina—how she was surely the last daughter anyone would ever have expected to abandon her parents to go to America. About her own children—would they have the patience for what lay ahead? And about her own aging body—when would it finally betray her?

"I'm not sure, Maria." Giovanna's voice trembled slightly. Maria could feel the trembling in Giovanna's hands as she grabbed them from the countertop and helped her to straighten up. And then suddenly the trembling was gone and Giovanna was grabbing the pan of food and walking to the table.

"It just happens sometimes. I get stuck." She half-laughed and put the pan on the table, brushing her hand in the air with an unconvincing blasé. "It's my aging body, I guess."

"Stress, no doubt." Big Antonio said. "You should tell the doctor at the medical center."

"Oh for God's sake, Antonio. He's a child," she answered. She looked at Maria as she began spooning the caponata into the bowls. "There's bread in the drawer. And why didn't you tell me about that new doctor? I thought it was still Michalina."

They all heard the distant ring of the phone as it wafted in through the back window.

"Twice in one day," Big Antonio pushed his chair back with such force it almost scrapped a small line in the stone floor. He was out the door before the second ring. Maria and Giovanna sat, each looking at a different place on the table, their ears alert and waiting while Pastore di Capre slurped noisily at his carbonata.

Giovanna put both hands on the edge of the table, ready to stand, waiting not so patiently. The ringing had stopped. She looked at Maria.

"Must not be Angelina." They both knew he'd be calling Giovanna's name if it were. But he did not return. It was a few minutes later, after they'd resumed their eating when Big Antonio came back into the kitchen and both women looked up at him.

"It was Angelina. She's going to call back in an hour."

"Why didn't you call me?" Giovanna did not try to hide her

irritation. She felt as though she'd missed an important moment that would never again repeat itself. It was an irrational sadness, she knew that, but she couldn't stop it from flowing through her veins. Her eyes welled up.

"Now wait a minute," Big Antonio began to panic.

Maria momentarily weighed her allegiance and then said, "What's wrong with you? You know she's been waiting." She threw her cloth napkin at him and it landed across one shoulder. It was enough of a distraction for Giovanna to compose herself and she felt the need to defend him. Her eyes were a bit wet but the tears had passed.

"It's okay. An hour is not so long," she said.

Big Antonio defended himself as he grabbed the napkin from his shoulder. "I didn't want you to run up," he said, "especially with that getting-stuck-thing that just happened. You might have fallen. You could have—"

Giovanna interrupted, "Oh no, Antonio! You didn't tell her, did you?"

He didn't answer. He looked quickly down at his bowl, picked up his spoon and began eating. One could not be expected to answer with a mouthful of food.

*   *   *   *

Angelina sat in the armchair next to the sofa staring at the pink dawn as it made its way through the apartment window above the hot plate. Patrice's cell phone lay in her lap where she'd let it fall after her conversation with her mother hours before. As Big Antonio had told her, she'd waited one hour, watching it, minute by minute, on the digital display of the cell phone, before redialing.

Pasquale lay on the couch, the blanket pulled up to his chin but he was awake. He hadn't slept at all since getting the kids up the stairs and realizing how they'd betrayed his trust.

"*This never would have happened on Incompresso,*" he thought, without realizing that it was on Incompresso that he had lost his son to the juvenile justice system.

"We can close the store today," he said with a yawn. "You can put a sign on the door. Make something up. A family emergency."

"Absolutely not!" Angelina was thinking of the money and the new worry that had been heaped upon her in that brief telephone call with Big Antonio. She walked slowly to the sofa and pulled Pasquale's feet up, sat on the lumpy cushion and put his feet on her lap.

"Pat we need the money."

"One day won't matter," he said. He had been the one who'd insisted on a seven-day work week for them all, saying it was temporary, believing that they'd be able to give Rocco a running start with the business and then go back and rest on Incompresso. But now that he saw the state both Patrice and Rocco had come home in, he began to rethink his position—and Javier's offer of a partnership. It was too much work. It was wearing the family down to a nub like balsa wood against a grindstone. He felt Angelina reach under the blanket and begin to gently rub the arch of his foot.

"I need to go back," she said softly. "I can't leave them there."

"What'd she say?" Pasquale was asking about the two telephone calls.

"Big Antonio—he thinks my mother is ill. He's not sure. He just said something about her hands shaking, something about her—" Angelina stopped and looked off into the distance at nothing. Her hand stopped rubbing. She squinted her eyes and looked down at Pasquale, "You know, during this last visit, I did notice her head—as she was watching television, it was sort of nodding, a really quick movement. I thought it was the music, but then the music stopped and . . . "

Pasquale asked, "What'd your mother say when you called

back?"

"Oh, you know her." Angelina was imitating her mother's singsong voice "Everything's fine. Don't worry. It's her nerves. Nothing's wrong la-di-da. What would we tell our kids, Pat—if it were us? What else could she say?" Angelina hesitated. "But she needs me there. I'm sure."

Pasquale quickly slid his feet to the floor and sat up, the blanket tangled around his waist. He looked at Angelina. "I need you here."

"Hire someone."

"How will I talk to him?"

"How about your cousin. He probably knows someone. An Italian."

"We cannot trust him—look at this mess?" Pasquale put his hand out and scanned the apartment. It was the first time he admitted his mistake—or at least alluded to it.

"Well, what am I suppose to do, Pat? *Your* parents are gone. You don't understand."

"Angelina, that's not fair. Your parents are mine too." He knew it wasn't true the minute it escaped his mouth. "Let's close the store today. All of us need a break. I'll talk to Javier. See if his offer still stands. Between Spanish and Italian and a bit of English, he's the only one I can talk to if you're not here."

"I don't know, Pat. You close the store one day and they go somewhere else. Can Javier work it alone?"

"I'll call him. Where's his number?"

"It's downstairs. But can he handle it?"

"He'll be fine. His daughter can help him. We can take the car to the shore. Discuss our options—a family meeting like we used to do when they were small." He smiled. "They're adults now. Their opinion—"

"Ach! They don't act like adults," Angelina stood up abruptly and spit the words, "What the hell was Rocco thinking?"

*　　　*　　　*　　　*

When Gina drove past the pizzeria on her way home from work, she saw the dark window and felt a pit of emptiness in her chest. Had she hurt the woman more than she realized? And was Rocco gone? In the twelve years she'd been driving past that store, to and from the hospital, she'd never seen it empty—not even when the ownership had changed two years ago. There'd been ladders in front of the ordering counter, workmen painting ceilings and pulling carpet up, yet they still somehow managed to maintain a flow of customers.

Gina parked in the driveway outside her empty house and almost didn't see her mother sitting on the porch stairs.

"Where's your car?" she asked as she closed her own car door and sat beside her mother on the rough cement step.

"It wouldn't start. Maybe it's the battery."

Her mother brushed the hair from Gina's cheek and kissed her gently. She put her arm around Gina as they sat side by side looking straight out at the blue sky.

"Your dad always took care of those things."

Now why did she have to say that? Why the first thing? She was expecting Gina to comfort her and yet Gina could barely find the words to converse with her mother.

"Well, how'd you get here?"

"Taxi."

"Really?" Gina looked at her mother. "We have taxis in Robin's Nest?"

"Sure. Well—it wasn't exactly from Robin's Nest, I don't think. I called a number I found on the computer and they sent a taxi. It's too far to walk."

"Why didn't you just call me? Or Joe?"

"I did. You didn't answer your phone. I thought maybe there

was something wrong with it."

Gina pulled her cell phone from her pocket, looked at the screen, and put it back in her pocket. "Oh, sorry. You should have just gone inside. It's too chilly out here. Forgot your key?"

"That alarm of yours, I don't want to trigger it."

Her daughter had shown her several times how to turn the alarm off. But the few times Delores had gone into the house alone, the urgent beeping made her nervous as she tried to punch the numbers into the alarm pad. And there was that time she entered the combination of numbers in the wrong order. The siren was deafening, not to mention embarrassing as she ran from the house with the neighbors looking on. The police officer who pulled up to the house intimidated her so much so that she almost thought she had done something criminal. No, it was too nerve-wracking. She'd rather sit outside and wait, even if it meant risking pneumonia.

Gina shook her head lightly. "Oh mom . . ."

"You still watch that talk show?" her mother asked, "The one at four 'o clock? There's a woman on today talking about bereavement." She looked at her watch, "Let's go inside. It started already."

"*Not interested,*" Gina thought.

As they rose from the step, her mother turned to her and said, "When is Joe going to take care of that branch?" She was looking at the jagged edges of the oak. "He can come and get the chainsaw anytime he wants."

Delores brushed away the dust from the back of her pants and added quietly, "It's all gassed up and ready, just sitting in the garage where dad left it." She waited for Gina to unlock the door. "I should have brought it with me."

"In a taxi, mom?" Gina was pushing the buttons to turn off the alarm. "You wouldn't have been able to lift it."

"The taxi driver could have. He was a lovely man. Jamaican—I think." She put her purse on the countertop. "His accent was so sweet. I'm not sure, though—some island somewhere. But he was a talker for sure. And I bet he would have lifted it for me."

"It's okay, mom. Joe will go get it."

As if on cue, they heard the sound of Joe's car pulling into the driveway.

Gina looked at her mother and then at her watch. "He's home early."

Joe came into the house with a big smile on his face that turned to confusion when he saw his mother-in-law.

"Delores?" It was half question, half greeting.

"Mom's car won't start. She thinks it's the battery."

"Oh," he came up to Gina and kissed her on the cheek. Gina waited, accepted it and then pulled away and went to the refrigerator door and opened it. She stood looking into it without moving. Joe watched her for a few seconds and then turned to his mother-in-law.

"I'll bring some jumper cables over. I don't know much about cars. If that doesn't work, we can tow it to the dealer's garage."

"You're a sweetheart, Joe." Delores was headed toward the sofa, her eyes searching for the television remote control.

Joe looked quickly from his mother-in-law to Gina who was still standing with one hand on the open refrigerator door, looking into it. He took a step toward Gina, stopped, turned and followed Delores to the sofa.

"Where's your remote?" she asked Joe as he came up behind her.

"Delores, I can drive you back now. I'll go get the jumper cables from the garage."

"Trying to get rid of me?" she laughed but stopped mid-laugh when she heard her question met with silence.

Joe's eyes swept past hers and looked at Gina and then back again to Delores. He swallowed.

"Oh no, uh—" He hesitated and they both turned to watch Gina as she closed the refrigerator and went to the sink. She stood and looked out the window, through the tree branches along the fence.

"Well, of course. I should take care of that." Delores was looking at Gina but Gina did not move. Her eyes searched beyond the branches. Her hands held the edge of the sink. She was alone in the house.

"It's just—well," Joe tried again, "you'll need the car tomorrow, and who knows how long it'll take and, uh, well."

"Okay, dear," Delores turned abruptly and walked into the kitchen toward Gina who appeared to have suddenly emerged from sleep.

Gina turned around and faced her mother, "Mom, you don't have to go. We'll have dinner together. I'll throw a pot of macaroni on. There's some—"

"Okay, uh," Joe walked up to the counter beside them and put his hand down on it, as if steadying himself. "Yeah, she's right, Delores. I can drive you after dinner. It's just that I had something to—well, never mind. It can wait."

Delores did not want to go back to her empty house. She understood the silent pleading from Joe but she ignored it.

"Great. I'll make something to put on the macaroni." She moved to the pantry door. "You have onions? I'll chop some up."

Gina shrugged and Joe disappeared into the hallway.

Delores opened the pantry door and moved the items around on the shelves as the two women listened to Joe's footsteps ascend the stairs and then shuffle above them on the second floor.

Dinner was slow and laborious—as Joe perceived it. For Delores, it was painfully quick and with the dishes in the dishwasher, the pots washed and dried, and the kitchen light extinguished, she knew it was time to leave.

Joe had his car keys in his jeans pocket. He pulled them out as he stood from the sofa and handed them to Delores.

"Here, take my car. Gina and I can drive together tomorrow." He looked at Gina, "if you don't mind going in early with me."

Gina was sitting on a stool at the kitchen counter looking at her telephone. She looked up and shrugged her shoulders. "Okay."

Delores saw no way out of it. Now she'd have both cars—hers and Joe's. Her plan to feign ignorance when Joe came and started her car, was still viable, had still allowed her the excuse of yet another evening outside of that empty house but now she'd inconvenienced Gina and that hadn't been her intention. She took the keys from her son-in-law.

"Thanks, Joe." She stood for a second without a word.

"We'll come over tomorrow night and jump your car, bring it to the garage," Joe said. "Maybe you can get a loaner from them."

"Okay." She turned to leave.

As Gina heard her mother's footsteps enter the hallway, she jumped from the stool. "Put the porch light on." She followed her mother.

Delores put her hand around Gina's waist, "You're too quiet. Are you okay? You barely ate."

"My stomach's funny. I'm okay."

"Well—what do we expect? It's only been a few months."

"Hm." Gina knew it'd been more than a year. She didn't bother to correct her mother. Instead she kissed her on the cheek and flipped the switch for the porch light as her mother opened the door. "I'm okay, mom."

"Saturday morning, if you want. I still go and it helps." Delores was talking about her bereavement support group.

"I don't think so."

"Is it because it's at the hospital?"

"Maybe. I don't know. I'm okay, don't worry."

Delores returned the kiss and then walked out the door. Gina started up the stairs but Joe was off the sofa in seconds and trotting down the hallway.

"Wait. Where are you going? I wanted to talk to you."

"I'm tired Joe."

He ascended the stairway behind her and followed her into the bedroom where he sat on the bed and watched her as she began to remove her work scrubs.

Joe practiced his opening line in his head. He had to get it right—so she'd actually hear him, rather than just agree with whatever he said, without attending to what he meant. He knew he'd almost completely lost her. This was his last chance.

It hadn't always been like this. He understood the stages of grief: denial, anger, bargaining, depression, and acceptance—nice and neat in a little packaged paradigm. He was a nurse after all; he'd learned them in a class and referred to them at the hospital's rehab center where the stroke patients mourned the loss of their limbs or language—where angry loved ones with no one to blame but the staff, listened to him drone on about something he'd never experienced. *Anger stage,* he'd think as he watched the wife of a patient stomp away. Neat and clean stages to walk through on the road to recovery.

But knowing something, having the educational background for the combat, having the professional experience for the need at hand, turned out to be not at all like fighting the battle itself— living within the paradigm.

Since Gina had identified her father's body at the morgue, since she'd slid into the abyss, Joe had found himself a helpless player on the other side of the coin. And now when he saw a grieving spouse, desperate for his partner to be who she used to be as each well-meaning professional tried to explain the changes of a damaged brain, Joe would listen helplessly—knowing no words were enough. He wanted the old Gina back—the one who'd come to the hospital twelve years before to do her internship.

He smiled as Gina tossed the blue scrubs into the hamper. Those scrub pants had no pleats at all. But it was that small gathering of cloth, the pleats that ran from the back of her knee up her leg and disappeared at the top of her thigh—the pleats on her scrubs twelve years before, that had drawn Joe to Gina. They brought his eye to her swaying buttocks as she followed her trainer, Peggy, to the nurses' station. He followed closely behind the two women, his eyes on the bunched up material at the back of Gina's pants as it swayed with her walk. And had those pants not had pleats, he'd never have met his wife but also he'd never have known that her pants were on backwards!

It was her first day and she had a *new-trainee* air about her as she followed Peggy.

"Joe, you have Mr. Ramirez's chart?" Peggy asked as she scanned the patients' charts in the nurses' station and then tilted her head back toward Gina.

"This is Gina." Her thumb pointed over her shoulder to indicate the girl in the backward pants and without looking at either of them, she said, "Gina, Joe."

When Gina turned to look at him, a warm pink hue filled her face. She took his extended hand and said "nice to meet you." But that color along with the coolness of her hand and the slight tremor in her voice, negated the self-assured look she tried to muster as their eyes met. And the backward pants totally obliterated it. Joe's intension was to tell her that she was wearing the scrub pants backwards but the momentum he'd had moments before as he'd followed her into the nurses' station, fizzled into dust when he met her gaze.

"Nice to meet you too," he said.

He looked at her now as she pulled the drawstring around a pair of pajama pants and he patted the bed where he sat.

"Come here a second."

"Joe, I'm tired. I'm not in the mood."

"God Gina, I don't want anything. Just to talk. I want to say something."

She sighed and sat next to him, her hands in her lap, her feet dangling off the side. He turned to her and said, "Look Gina." He gently touched the side of her face and guided her head toward him. She was looking down at her hands but suddenly looked up at him, seeing him for the first time in months, and she was filled with guilt, enough so that she gave him her full attention.

"I talked to Anast." Anast was a friend of theirs but also the head of personnel at the hospital rehab center. "We can get two weeks off together. I want to book a trip. Let's finally have that honeymoon. We can make it Italy—your father's area—like you've always wanted."

"Italy? Hmm." That seemed far enough away from Robin's Nest and it tugged at her heart when she thought of the number of times her father had said he wanted to go back.

He'd left as a child and barely remembered it. So why didn't he, then? Go back? What stopped him? He probably thought he had plenty of time. He'd planned the trip a few hundred times with her mother. Delores had been enamored by the idea and had gone to the travel agent, brought home brochures, and looked at possible flights on her laptop as her husband snored beside her in bed. But then they'd decided to wait until after Gina and her sister, Carmen, finished the university, then after the weddings were paid off, and then after his retirement—only two years away.

No one ever believes there's an expiration date on life, not until faced with the death of a peer and that simply had not yet happened to her father. He was the first of his friends, the first of his brothers, the first for Gina. She, herself, never had the misfortune of a friend or colleague's funeral. Her grandparents had both died when she was small and she hadn't attended that funeral. They were just gone. She hadn't any understanding of *death*.

So her father's was such a shock. He was supposed to grow old and feeble, to be a grandfather to the children she'd yet to have. He'd said he wanted to be called *Nonno*, grandfather in Italian, like he'd called his grandfather who'd lived with his *nonna* behind the family house, in their garage-turned-apartment on the shore.

Gina's father was so excited after his daughters married. He not-so-patiently awaited the grandchildren—not *grandchild* for he was certain there'd be more than just one. He'd planned to take them to the beach and to the park and to the candy store like the grandfathers on television. And he had stories of the old country he wanted to tell them, the way his *nonno* had told him—though Gina's father couldn't remember a thing about the old village, but still it would be his grandchildren's roots, their identity. Children need to know who they are. He'd meant to do it with his own daughters, but then there was work and time got away from him, and well he hadn't married an Italian like the rest of his family. Maybe if he'd married an Italian. But with the grandchildren it would be different. He'd be the one to take the lead and teach them about their heritage. It was a promise he'd made to himself.

When his first daughter, Carmen, became pregnant, it was a joyous moment—to know that he was getting that second chance to be a father by way of grandfather-hood. Her belly grew and so did his anticipation.

And when Carmen moved away—too far for the fantasy-grandfather-plan, he'd put all his hope in Gina. But now he was gone. And since his death, the thought of children petrified her. Look how easily they could be left alone in the world. No—it was for the best—no children for her and she did what she could to keep Joe at bay.

Now Gina thought about Joe's proposal for a trip to Italy. She thought of her mother and about her sister's move to California. Did it feel better out there? Was it easier to become someone else in a new location, than be who she had to be here in Robin's Nest? Maybe that's what she needed—a new location. Gina was mulling it over as she looked into Joe's eyes without seeing him. She saw the nurse's station crowded with files of patients whose daughters were caught between their own life and the new one handed to them, with a broken parent. She saw the therapy room, overrun with materials for the newly disabled, books and props looking professional and useful, sitting impotent on shelves and tables. She saw her father's gray waxy face as the morgue drawer was pushed back into place. And she saw the dark windows of the pizzeria.

"Yeah." She nodded her head and reentered the world where Joe sat waiting. "Yeah, okay."

Joe exhaled, not realizing he'd been holding his breath. His smile stretched from ear to ear.

"I'll take care of everything—for the trip I mean. You don't have to do anything. But I was thinking." He inhaled deeply again. "Maybe you could call your sister, Carmen. It would be good if your mother spent that time with her in California. You think she'd go for it?"

"I have no idea. I'll give it a try. I'd rather not have to worry about her—here alone."

The guilt from Gina's last encounter with her father, before he'd headed to the hunting lodge to secure it from the fugitives, was a guilt that dissolved her bones and ate at her organs as the last words they'd spoken together rested its weight against her throat. She could not endure even the slightest increase, not one more ounce of it. The idea of her mother tucked safely somewhere—vacation or no vacation—appealed to her greatly.

"I'll call Carmen. What time is it in California?" She looked at her watch. "She's probably still at work. I'll call in a little while.

CHAPTER 7

Pasquale parked the car behind the pizzeria and cut the engine as the others opened the doors to get out. The trip to the shore had been exactly as he'd hoped. They were a family again. Rocco and Patrice seemed closer than ever, whispering in the back seat all the way there, laughing at whatever private joke they'd shared. It was as if they were back on the island. Pasquale was the driver with his beautiful bride beside him as she commented on the scenery and gently rubbed his shoulder now and then.

Angelina had to agree. They all seemed happier than they'd been since the day they'd been reunited in Robin's Nest, especially the children. Well, certainly they were no longer children, but it felt as if they were again. Just for that one afternoon she'd had them back.

If she didn't look behind her now, at the two adults sitting side by side in the back seat, she could fool herself into feeling the presence of little Patrice and Rocco, eight years old and fifteen. Before their world had imploded. She put a hand on her chest, and she felt a longing for those early years — so much so that she hesitated to look back at the two as Patrice addressed her.

"You want this sweater, Mama?" Patrice was holding a sweater toward her mother as Rocco opened the door to get out of the car and Angelina reached back and took it without looking.

"Mama," she thought, *"I'll always be Mama."* She smiled and brought her feet to the asphalt as she left the car and then — poof — she was back in Robin's Nest and her small children had disappeared into vapor, leaving in their place a gangly pair of somewhat-adults walking toward the back entrance.

Inside the dimly lit foyer, at the foot of the stairs, Pasquale turned to Rocco and said, "Come into the store. Let's just make sure there's enough dough for tomorrow." He put his key into the newly-replaced lock of the door leading to the back of the kitchen as Patrice and Angelina walked up the stairs to the apartment.

Both Pasquale and Rocco were alit with the sweetness of the day. It had been a good one, something to which they both would have agreed if asked. And there hadn't been much agreement between them for some time. Rocco followed his father from the kitchen through the small swinging door, out into the darkened store. He looked behind at the kitchen as the door swung shut.

"I thought you wanted to check the dough," he said.

"Yeah, uh I do." Pasquale answered, "but let's sit here for a moment first."

He sat at a table near the back wall. The warm twilight shone through the front window and washed his son's face with hope. Rocco hesitated and then slid into the seat across from his father.

"Oh, uh — do you want something to drink?" Pasquale asked as if it suddenly occurred to him as he sat with his hands on the tabletop.

Rocco shook his head, "What's going on?"

"What? I can't talk to my son? I just want a minute without the girls. I want to discuss the store — just you and me."

Rocco shrugged his shoulders. "Okay, so?"

"It was a nice day, wasn't it?" Pasquale started and Rocco nodded. He agreed. It felt good at the sea — familiar and soothing.

"Yeah," Rocco said, "Nice. It reminded me of home."

Pasquale continued, "Listen, you can go back to the island if you want or you can stay here. It's just that I thought, you know —

since you got out—that well, the island was kind of uh," he scratched his chin, "small for you?"

Rocco nodded slowly. "You're embarrassed, aren't you? Your son, the convict—I get it."

"No! Not true, Rocco. I always understood what happened, and if it had been a hundred years ago, you'd have been hailed a hero—even Nonno Pastore agreed with you. You know that. But it's not a hundred years ago, and well, there was nothing we could do. It was so far from home."

Rocco looked down at his hands and began picking at his thumbnail as Pasquale continued. "I was grooming that herd of goats for you. It was getting bigger, more kids each spring—I thought maybe we could export—something like, well, I was preparing it for *you*. But the car, Rocco, the stolen car. Why?"

"Ach," Rocco balled both hands into fists and hit the table hard causing Pasquale to startle and push himself back on the seat.

"Again with this?" Rocco said and opened his clenched teeth letting out enough of a sigh that Pasquale felt it in his face. "This is what you want to talk about?" Rocco put his hands on the table's edge ready to push himself out from the table.

"No, no, wait." Pasquale put his hand on Rocco's arm. "Stay, it's not what I wanted to say. I want to tell you about the store."

"What about it?" Rocco settled a bit.

"Javier is going to become a partner. I talked to him on the phone this morning. We're going to look at the profits and talk to a lawyer. He's going to buy his way in. We'll have a sum of money. And well—we're thinking, your mother and I, we've talked about buying a house—maybe behind the store." Pasquale nodded toward the kitchen. "Those houses back there are small— maybe," his voice trailed off and Rocco remembered what Patrice had told him the night before about those houses. He thought of the woman in the blue sedan—*Jane*.

"But then," Rocco hesitated. "A partner? You trust him, Javier? I mean, he's a good guy but what about me? I know I can't have my name on the store without proper immigration papers. But what about Javier's?"

"We'll see a lawyer. Maybe I can sponsor him. I'm not sure how it works but we're going to try."

Pasquale didn't mention the idea that a man such as Javier without a criminal record, without so much as a speeding ticket, an upstanding gentleman with a family had more of a chance for success than that of Rocco who'd forfeited such opportunity the day he'd become a murderer at fifteen. It wasn't necessary. It was understood.

Rocco continued, "But if something happens to you—what about me? And how about the profits? We'll have to share them. I don't know about this. What'd Mama think?"

"She's in agreement. The house is a big part of it and, well— Nonna Giovanna is having some problems."

"How will a house here, help Nonna? Why not take the money back there—it'll go further. I thought that was always the plan."

"That's an idea." But not one that Pasquale was interested in anymore—not after Angelina's conversation with her mother.

Incompresso had been there for thousands of years. It wasn't going anywhere. He'd go back to visit when he could, but for now he was interested in getting his son on track, giving him a life that they all could be proud of, but also in satisfying Angelina's need to help her parents.

Pasquale saw that Rocco had softened a bit so he continued, but tread lightly, hoping to maintain the calmer conversation.

"We can talk about that later. For now, though—I wanted you to know what was happening with the store."

Rocco nodded. "Okay—I get it," he said. "I'm going upstairs. You check the dough. You don't need me for that."

He got up and walked through the kitchen door. Pasquale watched the back of his son flicker away as the kitchen door swung in and out a few times and then he heard the back door close and the dull thud of Rocco sprinting up to the apartment. He sat back in the chair and stared at the empty seat across the table.

Patrice was standing at the window near the hot plate when Rocco reached the landing and walked through the open door.

"Did he tell you about the house idea?" she asked.

He nodded. "When are you going to see Josh again?"

He wanted that feeling back—the freedom, the fun and laughter, the escape from memories of the boy's camp, the jail, and his own ugly thoughts.

"Not soon enough," Patrice answered, and she was glad to have Rocco in on her relationship with Josh. She pulled her telephone out of her front pocket and looked at the screen.

Her finger poked at it a few times and Rocco knew she'd left again, escaped the pizzeria, the apartment—she was gone. He watched her poke a few more times. Smile. Poke-poke-poke. Shake her head lightly. Bigger smile. Poke-poke.

"What?" Rocco cocked his head and she looked up at him.

"Oh, nothing."

"Well? What's he saying?"

"No. It wasn't Josh. He didn't answer me yet. I told him to come by the pizzeria tomorrow."

"It wasn't Josh?"

She shook her head but didn't say anything else. Her head went down again, the blue screen reflected in her eyes. It was a portal, an opening to the rest of the world. She was Alice sailing down the rabbit hole, Dorothy on the yellow brick road, Persephone wandering through the underworld.

Rocco went into his bedroom and stood at the foot of the bed. He looked around at the empty room—one bed, one dresser, one small closet missing a door and packed with possessions. He could use a bit of that escape right now, he thought. He paced back and forth and then went back in the living area where Patrice stood as still as a stone staring into the telephone screen. His mother came out of the bathroom.

"What's wrong?" Rocco's restlessness filled the room.

Patrice looked up. She looked from her mother to Rocco and then went into the bedroom she share with Angelina and closed the door.

Angelina came close to her son. "What's wrong, Rocco?"

"Nothing. I just thought, maybe," he looked around the room. "I was looking for," he hesitated, bent down and opened the refrigerator under the hotplate. "I was going to have a beer." The refrigerator had a carton of milk, a bag of coffee beans and a half-eaten chocolate bar. Nothing else. "I just thought to relax a bit with a beer."

"Get one from downstairs."

Angelina watched him carefully as he shut the refrigerator and straightened his body. His head came to the window over the hotplate and he looked out over the darkening sky.

"So you and Papa—you discussed Javier?"

"Yeah."

She waited.

"You want one?" Rocco walked to the apartment door, "A beer?"

She shook her head and he disappeared out the door.

Angelina walked over to the little refrigerator and felt in the space next to the wall for the bottle of grappa her mother had given her. She pulled it from its place and walked into the bathroom, closing the door without a sound. She opened the bottle and took a long gulp, then emptied its contents into the toilet and threw the empty bottle into the bathroom trash. She stood looking at it for a few seconds before she bent over and pushed it further into the trash bin and threw some paper towels over it.

*   *   *   *   *

When Josh walked into the pizzeria the next day, Rocco might have been happier than Patrice to see him. They both lit up as he came to the counter. He was wearing his mechanic's uniform and Patrice thought it made him look even more handsome. Their father noticed Josh too, but didn't recognize him as someone who'd been to the store several times. It was actually Rocco's reaction that caused Pasquale to take note.

"Hey, Josh!" Rocco wiped his hands on his apron and came around the counter. "Hey buddy, stay for a while. Go sit back there. No charge for you. What do you want?"

"Get back in your cage, monkey." Patrice elbowed him, "I take care of the customers."

Patrice led Josh to the empty table next to the kitchen. The table had small boxes and folded napkins stacked high. It wasn't meant for customers.

"It's kind of a busy time, but I can talk for a minute."

"You look beautiful."

"Oh." Patrice wasn't used to compliments. "So do you." She smiled and pulled a piece of hair behind her ear.

Josh was suddenly looking over her shoulder so she turned to see her brother approaching the table with a slice of pizza. Patrice rolled her eyes.

"I can take care of this," she said to Rocco, "get out of here. Go help Papa."

The telephone by the cash register began ringing. They both looked at it and then saw their father watching.

"I'll be right back." Patrice said to Josh as she pushed her brother toward the front, "Go help Papa before he has a fit." The telephone continued to ring.

Rocco ignored her and stood next to Josh still holding a soggy paper plate with a slice of pizza as his sister retreated toward the front. The telephone rang again and Angelina flew out of the kitchen door with a furrowed brow, just as Patrice picked up the receiver. She looked at Josh and then at Rocco who wasn't sure what to say so he introduced Josh.

Angelina's mouth said, "nice to meet you," but her eyes on

Rocco said, *"What the hell are you doing?"* She saw Pasquale watching as he threw the pizza dough into the air.

"Go help you father, honey." She said it with a smile and then looked at Josh, "And Patrice will come and help you."

"Why is he sitting at this table?" she said in Italian, still smiling but her lips were pulled so tightly together it barely had the right to be labeled a smile.

"I got it, Mama. Go back in the kitchen."

She shook her head slowly, still smiling, but to Josh it was obvious by the switch to Italian and the electricity pulsing from her eyes that this was not some sweet banter between mother and son.

"Papa needs your help." Angelina sensed that this intruder was somehow related to the state in which her children had returned home the night before.

"I gotta go anyway." Josh stood up and grabbed the paper plate. "Thanks." He was looking past them both at Patrice who was at the register taking care of a customer and returning his gaze.

"Wait." Rocco said.

"It was nice meeting you, Josh." Angelina said his name as though it were a lemon wedge in her mouth. And to Rocco she said, "Rocco, you — " There was more to her sentence but he was ignoring her and following Josh up to the register.

Patrice walked from the register to the pizza oven to retrieve a box above it. She was still looking at Josh as he passed by the register.

"Text me," she whispered and he understood her lips and nodded as Rocco followed him out the door.

Both Pasquale and Patrice watched as the two young men exchanged a few words and nods and then Rocco patted him on the back and stepped back into the store, visibly pleased with himself. Pasquale didn't know what to make of it but felt a pang of relief to see his son smiling.

No one noticed Josh drive around the side and to the back of the store. But they all saw Gina. She was walking away from her car, toward them.

Gina had seen Rocco outside the store as she pulled into the parking lot. It was the first time she'd seen him outside in the daylight. Yes, he was much younger than she, she could see that then. His smile as he patted the other young man on the back, showed a smooth lip line, a warm light in his eyes. Gina sat in her car for a moment and watched them in her rearview mirror as her hands gripped the steering wheel, though the car was no longer running and did not need steering.

What was it about this guy? She watched Rocco absently roll up his sleeves—the muscles in one arm pulsing as his hand reached for the door and pushed it inward. Gina's hands dropped from the steering wheel. She opened the car door and remembered to exhale and to continue breathing.

It was a relief to see the store lit and alive with movement. As much as she longed for change, she was relieved to see the status quo had returned—the buzz of customers, the heat of the ovens, the older man working at the counter, and Patrice's smile as she greeted Gina—all welcome familiarity.

"Hey *Jane*, how are you? You didn't call in an order, did you?" Patrice searched her memory and then started looking at the screen on the register for her order. How had she missed it?

Pasquale wiped his hands on his apron and made his way toward the kitchen.

"No." Gina said, "Actually, I came to see if your mother was all right?"

"My, mother?" Patrice was confused.

"Doesn't matter," Rocco said, "We can make you whatever you want." And he watched Gina's face redden as she looked at him, her head slightly bent, her eyes deep and woeful and expressing something Rocco could not figure out as it sailed toward him. But it helped him regain his power after the humiliation in the bar and he quite liked it. "What is it you want, *Jane*? Tell me."

"Just your mother," Gina hesitated.

The words were suddenly stuck in her throat. "I was—we met the other day. I just wanted . . . "

Her face got warmer. Rocco watched the red blotches appear, one at a time and then run down the skin on her neck and disappear into her blue scrub shirt. He smiled. He wanted to touch her and see what else his power could produce.

"I'll make it for you. What is it you want?" he asked.

"Gina?" Angelina was coming out of the kitchen door with Pasquale following her. Gina's reddened face and Rocco's lit smile did not escape her.

"Gina, how are you?"

Patrice looked from her mother to the customer standing before her. "Gina?" Her mother was mistaken. "Mama, it's *Jane*. You know."

"Yes, okay. You have her name wrong." Patrice and Rocco looked at each other and then at Gina as she stuttered her way to a greeting.

"Angelina—oh, uh hi—I just wanted, um." Suddenly she felt Angelina's accusation as the older woman looked at her and then at Rocco.

"*No, no.*" Gina thought, "*It's not him.*" But her red face betrayed her even if her intentions had been pure. She said, "I was worried when I saw the store closed yesterday." Gina pressed her lips together, "*No, wait—it sounds like I'm watching their every move.*" She tried again. "I drive past here to go to work. I happened to see you were closed."

"We're open now," Rocco interrupted her, "Ready to serve you."

But his mother's look as she turned briefly toward him and then back to Gina, silenced him. His power fizzled into the air and it angered him.

Gina saw the exchange as she looked toward Rocco and then

caught Angelina's consternation as she turned back to his mother.

"Actually, I just wanted to be sure you were okay. You know, after the other day — "

"I'm fine."

"The other day?" Both Rocco and Patrice had the same thought.

"Great." Gina said. The store was no longer where she wanted to be. She turned and ignored Rocco's gaze as she pushed past a few customers and walked quickly to her car.

As Gina slid onto the front seat and closed the car door Rocco felt a tightness in his chest, a loss he hadn't felt since the day his mother wiped away his tears, kissed his forehead and handed him back to the guards at the boys' camp. But it wasn't something he consciously picked apart and analyzed. It was a feeling, a sense of helplessness. It opened a place inside his chest where a monstrous anger threatened to emerge, and the instinct to fight it back, to push it down into place and bury it deep, struggled for control.

Rocco turned to the counter beside his father, grabbed a ball of dough and punched it into the counter. He was going to flatten it out and begin throwing it but the punch had more force than he had intended and he felt his knuckles crush against the wooden block. They split open and spilled blood into the dough.

"What are you doing?" Pasquale said quietly as he grabbed Rocco's wrist to stop the second blow. Then he pulled a towel from the shelf near his head and threw it over the bloody dough and battered knuckles.

"Stop," Pasqual whispered loudly as he held both of Rocco's balled up fists, the towel between them. "Please." He pushed against Rocco's hands as they fought to come up again. "Rocco, no."

Pasquale felt his son's body begin to relax as he pulled the towel around his hands, some of the dough caught within.

"Go wash your hands in the kitchen." Pasquale was still talking quietly as Rocco pulled the towel and gathered it over his battered fists. He looked at his father and saw the panic in his eyes. He looked back down at his hands wrapped in the towel and then at his mother who was watching as she brought a pizza box to a customer who seemed unaware of what was happening behind the counter, near the ovens. Rocco saw the look of fear pass between his parents. He put his head down in shame and walked to the kitchen.

"Tell Javier to come out." Angelina said, "*You* can stay in there and cook." Javier often prepared the toppings and the side dishes.

In the kitchen, Rocco plunged his fists into the sink's soapy water, along with the towel and pizza dough. Javier left him there. Rocco pulled the plug out of the drain, and then pulled his battered hands from the water. He watched the water trickle down the drain as he turned on the faucet and put his hands under the cold water. Leaning against the metal side of the sink, he stared at the faucet.

The icy cold water running over his knuckles numbed his hands as the stream from the faucet numbed his mind. Rocco stared at the line of water as it twisted and turned in its steady flow, until it moved like a living being and the metal sink blurred into blackness. He was staring into the spring water back home on the island. It was the rocky edges of the opening where the water gushed from the stones and fell into a perfect line of silver. He was perched at the top of the ridge—the one he used to climb while his father herded the goats. It was boredom that always brought him to that waterfall, boredom that hatched the stowaway plan on the ferry, and boredom that ensnared him in its deceptive net of painfully poor decisions.

From the height of the ridge he could turn and watch the ferry as it left the dock below. It was as small as his thumb and he made an imaginary line to the mainland of Italy's heel, which was a thick grayness on the horizon. The day was crisp and dry. He could see small white blotches that he knew were houses and stores and the harbormaster's quarters. They were structures that held people's lives and he felt a pang that hadn't been there on the other days. So on that day, not long after he'd turned fifteen, as he followed the line on the horizon—his mind fueled by a curiosity that had previously been more fantasy than plan—he decided he'd go to the other side and see it alone. Well, not exactly alone, but rather without his father or his mother at his side.

He'd been there plenty of times, mostly to the port. There were hardware stores and ironworks that his father liked to visit. It's where Pasquale had ordered the grating for their fireplace. And Rocco had accompanied him on many trips to listen to his father speak with the blacksmith and to make suggestions to certain designs that lay around the shop though none were about his own fireplace grating.

Angelina could see no reason for such a grating. She was perfectly content with having the wood sit at the bottom of the fireplace. And the one Pasquale had ordered wasn't a plain iron bed on which to place the wood as Angelina had suggested. No, it had curves and fancy cutouts—much too ornate for the simple home they lived in. But Angelina had understood her husband's need to be where he wanted to be, rather than accept where he was. She'd felt there was no harm in the visits or the expensive fireplace grating. She understood.

For Rocco, in addition to the mainland port, there was only one other place he knew: the big airport, inland. It was the furthest he'd ever been from the island and it had happened only a few months before his fifteenth birthday. He'd accompanied Angelina to meet her friend, Jennifer, from England—Miss Jennifer to him. Miss Jennifer had brought with her a son, two years younger than Rocco. And that younger child had been on an airplane, was then in a new country and according to the conversations the two boys had had, Miss Jennifer's son was often in both an airplane and a new country—for his mother loved to travel and by extension, so did he.

Rocco and Miss Jennifer's son got on well together and a plan was construed between the two mothers in which Rocco would travel with Angelina back to England the following month. It was an exciting plan—one that Angelina had hoped for since the year she'd spent in Miss Jennifer's house as a sixteen-year-old student on her way to greatness. It had been with a few other girls her age that Father Marco had recognized as unique in intellect and he'd worked out a student program between churches. There were more formal ways of initiating such a program, but Father Marco knew an Italian priest who'd settled in a London church. The friendship between the two priests allowed them to set up that more informal student program. And it was a great opportunity. For Angelina it was a freedom she'd never felt and she was sure that she'd never return to the island. But that was before the London shooting that frightened Father Marco and the girls' parents enough to call them all back home to the safety of the island.

So fifteen-year-old Rocco awaited his visit to London with his mother, the airline tickets purchased and sitting atop the small table in his parents' bedroom. He felt a worldliness that came from the direct hit of sunlight on his barely clad torso—the heat of the stones beneath him toasting him into a drowsy adolescence as he left his childhood behind and watched the ferry draw her white line in the sea from the mainland.

He explained to the other boys how they could board unnoticed, for the ferry captain would surely mention it to at least one of their parents, as they were well known to him. The captain always had a short visit at the tavern before the ferry made her return to the mainland and one of the boys was Chair's grandson. If Rocco's plan was to work, if they were to be safely on board when the ferry left port, it would have to be that they were undetected or Chair would surely come aboard and lead his grandson by the ear off the ferry with the other boys following.

Oh, the memory of it! Success is a sweet and dizzying elixir. And his plan was certainly a success. But that success, that harmless diversion from the monotony of the island ended up leaving such a wake of destruction. Remembering the events of that day made it hard not to see the world as one random moment after another where Luck was the only driver. And it may have been Luck that led young Rocco and his friends aboard the ferry undetected, but she certainly abandoned them soon after.

Rocco's hands were numb from the ice-cold water. He reached up and turned off the faucet and then held the edge of the sink, overwhelmed by a fullness in his throat that seemed to cut off his airway. The walls in the kitchen grew smaller and darker. Air. He needed air. Without feeling the floor beneath his feet, he moved away from the sink and then into the back hallway and then out into the back parking lot. As the door slammed behind him, his lungs filled. He bent forward with his hands on his knees—gasping.

The back lot was empty except for his father's car and the dumpster. Rocco stood up straight and walked toward the back fence where the roofs of the houses peeked through the tree branches. There was movement in one window directly behind the elm that was positioned next to the dumpster but it wasn't the window that had his attention. He looked from side to side at the empty blacktop that stretched from one corner of the building to the other. Then he walked straight to the side of the dumpster. One more sweeping look from side to side and then a quick glance behind him before he ventured behind the dumpster and saw what he had hoped would be there.

As it turned out, Josh was a person who kept his word. He couldn't help it. It's how he wanted others to treat him, so he just naturally gravitated toward reliability and competence. His friends knew his character, knew if he made a promise to them, the deed was as good as done. But he was stingy with promises so Rocco hadn't known the value of it when Josh had answered his badgering with, "Yes. I promise, right now," as they stood together in front of the store. But Josh had said this with one thought in mind. Patrice. He wanted this brother of hers to be an ally, to say to Patrice who spent most of her waking hours with him, what a great guy Josh was. Respectable. Reliable.

And so there it was. The silver packet lay in the dirt next to the elm, a rock holding it down, lest a breeze should happen by before Rocco got to it, blowing it out of sight and rendering Josh unreliable—a liar.

Rocco had wanted more of that delicious escape he'd had with his sister and Josh, the other night. Whatever the substance was, cannabis or fairy dust, he didn't care. He just wanted to ease the tightness in his throat. He'd mistakenly thought the cannabis was something Josh had access to all the time. But Josh was just trying to figure out how to impress Patrice when he'd bought the small bag of weed from a friend of a friend. That foil packet of K-2 was still in his glove compartment but he'd never done it and he wasn't sure of the result. He couldn't guarantee it would be what Rocco wanted. No promises—except for its delivery behind the dumpster as Rocco had asked.

Rocco heard the door slam before he heard his mother's voice. He grabbed the K-2 packet and shoved it in his back pocket, then sat on the grass below the elm.

"What's happening with you, Rocco?" Angelina walked toward him. "Are you okay?"

Her voice was smooth, and it soothed Rocco almost as much as the foil packet in is back pocket. Just knowing he had the means of escape was enough to quiet his racing heart and open the airways to his lungs. Escape was possible, if not at that moment, then at some time in the near future.

Cement walls had never been the worst of his imprisonment. Rather it was that loss of control, the hopelessness of confinement, imagined or real. He felt the K-2 packet between him and the grass and it was enough. The possibility—it was enough.

Rocco exhaled loudly as Angelina sat beside him, "I'm okay." He looked at his mother. "Just needed a moment." That's what the doctor on television had said to the sobbing mother about her son.

It worked.

Angelina reached over and put her arm around Rocco. They both looked toward the back of the store. "It's hard. I know. It'll get easier."

But he wasn't sure what she meant. What would get easier — the memories, the fear, the pizza business? "Mama, what ever happened to Miss Jennifer?" he asked.

Angelina smiled. "Nothing, really. She got a little bit older probably. What made you think of her?"

"I don't know. I was thinking of that kid of hers. What was his name?"

"Roger?"

"Yeah, that's right. He was a good kid. We had some fun together." Rocco's insides began to churn again. How would his life have been different if they'd made that trip to England, if he'd never hatched the stowaway plan on the ferry?

"Oh, your father wasn't too crazy about either of them." Angelina sensed her son's apprehension. She knew that regret was as useless as sand in a desert.

"Really?" Rocco looked at his mother. "I didn't know that."

"Oh you were too young. Jennifer wasn't married and made no apologies about it. Your father used to call Roger, *the little bastard*, only to me, of course. I think he felt a bit threatened by her. A woman making her own money and having a child without any thought of a man? On Incompresso? She may as well have been a Martian."

"How did you convince him to let her come?"

"I never told him." She shook her head. "Wasn't my brightest moment. I knew he wouldn't agree to the visit so I pretended it was a surprise. They just showed up at the airport and needed us to come and get them. He figured it out. That's why he didn't come with us to greet them."

"Hm." So his mother had lied, deceived his father. He'd thought they were perfect together. Then again, he hadn't been there for most of their arguments, which had been predominantly about him.

Pasquale had often pointed to Jennifer as the influence that had taken his son down. Though Roger—having been *a little bastard* being raised by an *unwed whore* (Pasquale's words)—had faired far better than his own son.

"We did have a great time with them, didn't we?" Angelina didn't wait for an answer. "That's where I'd wanted to go, instead of here. She had offered to help us. Your papa wouldn't even consider it."

Angelina was about to stand up when Javier appeared at the back door. "Hey—we're busy in here." He smiled but he was obviously irritated, "Come on—what's going on?" He'd become a bit more assertive with the news that he might, after all, get the partnership he'd hoped for.

Angelina waved the back of her hand toward him and stood. "We're coming." She offered her hand to her son, "He's right. Let's get back in there."

Rocco accepted her hand and got up. He patted his back pocket and followed her into the store.

Gina had just arrived home and had been standing at her bedroom window when Rocco's movement at the back door of the restaurant had caught her eye. She watched as Rocco pushed his way out and bent over with his hands on his knees. She fought the instinct to open the window and call to him and then he moved closer to the fence and out of her view. She could see some movement between the slats of the wooden fence, next to the dumpster but she couldn't see what he was doing. He hadn't brought trash with him to dump there and he'd seemed somewhat distressed.

When Angelina came out, Gina was relieved to see someone there to help him and then she was lost in her own head hearing a conversation between mother and son that was made of stale air.

"I must be with her, mother. I don't care what the consequences are."

"Yes, son. She is a wonderful woman. You must go to her."

"I cannot wait."

"No, son – you shouldn't wait. Take her away from here."

"Yes! That's what I'll do. We will live in a castle on the moor and live off the land." Gina had recently read a Bronte book and couldn't quite conjure the backdrop of anywhere else.

"Go to her, son – she needs you."

"I'm going to her now, mother." Rocco's head appeared at the top of the fence as he began to climb over it.

"Gina! Where are you? Gina! I'm coming for you."

Gina opened the window. Her closely cropped brown hair was suddenly long flowing waves of spun gold that reached into the air and blew on the breeze. Rocco was over the fence and climbing up the side of the house as if he had suction cups on his feet. Gina pulled him into the window. He looked remarkably like a mixture of Joe and a prince from one of her childhood picture books.

They embraced.

"Oh, Gina."

"Oh Rocco."

"Hey! We're busy in here!" It was Javier's voice that brought her back to the place she had no desire to be and she stepped away from the window embarrassed by her own thoughts.

When Joe came home a few hours later, Gina was sitting on a stool with her laptop open on the kitchen counter. Images of the Mediterranean Sea were on the screen and Joe thought that was a good sign, Gina actively participating in their travel plans. He threw his jacket on the sofa and sat next to her.

"You're so late." She said as she glanced at the clock on the cooking range.

"They needed me in emergency. They were short a few hands."

"Car accident?" Gina continued scrolling through images of Italy's coastline.

Joe sighed. "That and the usual stuff—K-2 again." He slowly deflated from the frustration of nursing the body of an overdosing patient, especially the young one that was brought in today.

But Gina's half-hearted conversation was the first she'd initiated in a long time. He latched tightly onto it and didn't want it to end. "You know, that stuff I was telling you about?"

Gina's face remained on the computer screen. Salerno, Venice, Naples scrolled before them both. No response.

"Geez Gina. This one looked about ten years old." Gina looked away from the computer screen.

"Ten?" she asked.

Joe sighed, "The chart said she was fourteen but she was a tiny little thing and to tell you the truth, she might not make it."

"Really? That bad?"

"Yeah. God—how will we ever raise a kid in this world?" Joe put his elbows on the counter and his head in his hands.

Gina closed the laptop and put her hand on Joe's back.

Bingo! Joe felt the warmth of it like a starved man with a crumb in his hand. He continued.

"It breaks my heart. The whole thing."

He peeked one eye out from his hands and saw Gina looking at him. He took his hands from his face and clasped them on the countertop.

Gina was overwhelmed with guilt. She'd been searching for some indication online of the pizza store's owners—their origin in Italy—and now with Joe beside her, she felt the weight and stupidity of her thoughts. Joe was still in the real world dealing with real issues and producing altruistic results. She thought of her father. He loved Joe and was so happy when the two had married.

Gina's hand moved back and forth on Joe's back. She was looking at him nodding but couldn't think of anything to say.

"The trip will help." She smiled.

A smile? That was something big.

"I talked to Anast again," Joe said. "We've got two weeks together. It's not till next month, though. But May is perfect—

don't you think?"

"An anniversary trip," Gina said. She put her hand on the closed laptop. "Joe, let me ask you a question."

"Yeah?" His eyes dug into hers. Hope flooded his veins. "What is it?"

"Do you like this hair color? You never said anything about it, really."

Not what he had expected, but it was something. "Yeah sure. It looks nice."

"But you never acknowledged it."

"Hair? We're talking about hair when I've told you a little girl almost died in my arms?" Joe thought.

"Well, Gina. I uh," he hesitated. *What was she looking for?* "I think you're great no matter what you do."

"Hm."

Wrong answer? "You'd be beautiful with any color hair."

"I was just wondering." Gina said. "That's all." And then she added, "I didn't make dinner." She looked over to the sink and Joe noticed the cutting board with an onion and a knife. "I got distracted."

"That's fine. Let's go out."

"I'm not in the mood." Gina got up from the stool. "Have a bowl of cereal or something."

Joe exhaled loudly. He pushed the stool back from the counter and sat for a moment staring at the cutting board as he listened to Gina retreat to the sofa and then the television came on. This walking on eggshells was wearing him out. But he was a patient man.

CHAPTER 8

Giovanna was right. It *was* Carlo's death that marked the beginning of Pastore di Capre's decline—but it wasn't the actual murder, itself. Killing Carlo had been easy. It had meant nothing to Pastore di Capre as he had killed several times before. The war had made him a murderer and Carlo's death was no different in his mind. It was simply another means for survival. He was protecting his family, his children that had yet to be born, children whose birth Carlo seemed determined to prevent. So when Pastore di Capre bashed his good friend's head into a bloody pulp, the only effect it had was that of relief. The threat was gone. He was free. Giovanna was free.

But had he not encountered the gypsy woman who set those actions in motion, he might never have known the cause of his and Giovanna's loss. It was she—the old gypsy—who told him of it one November evening two years after the men had walked down the gangplank of the ferryboat with a few goats trailing them and a pouch full of gold coins.

Pastore di Capre could have ignored her as he had done all his life but when she mentioned the gold, he knew the lines in his hands were revealing more than they should have and her palm reading wasn't just a ploy for a couple of lira. He pulled his hand from her grasp and threw the coins at her.

"You're finished. Go away," he'd said to her.

Pastore di Capre and Carlo had left the goats in their shed on the mountain peak and they were sitting in the tavern before heading home. The milk cans were resting at their feet. At home, a pregnant Giovanna, her third attempt at a first child, awaited the men with a warm meal. After dinner, Carlo would retire to his apartment above the fruit seller's store and Pastore di Capre would enjoy a few moments with his wife before going to bed. In the morning, the two men would meet at the church to make the climb to the goat shed together. That was their routine. Giovanna accepted it but kept one eye searching for a suitable bride for Carlo for it was her belief that he spent too much time with her and her new husband, though Pastore di Capre didn't seem to agree.

For Pastore di Capre, life had steadily improved. He'd married Giovanna shortly after his return to the island and memories of the war and of Carlo's sisters faded to the back of his mind — though they never quite disappeared. No, they would never leave him, though eventually they'd lose their detail and become more of a hazy web of images.

But there in the tavern, the gypsy's words had shaken the life he'd made and completely rattled him, as she held his hand open and looked closely at the lines.

"You've taken something that's not yours," she said and she felt the hand tense ever so slightly. She licked her lips slowly, "it's valuable." She looked up briefly into Pastore di Capre's eyes. He didn't move, didn't blink. He just waited for her to continue.

Carlo had had a bit more grappa than Pastore di Capre, as was his usually habit. He heard the gypsy's accusation and joked.

"Hey, where's my pocket watch?" He laughed as he felt his pocket, "Is that what you've taken, Pastore?" And he took another sip of his drink.

Pastore di Capre's eyes remained on the gypsy woman. The old woman continued. "This is not a pocket watch," she said. "This is more valuable." His hand twitched a bit. "Gold," she said, "I see gold in this hand." And Pastore di Capre pulled his hand quickly from her grasp and pushed the lira on the table toward her.

"You're finished. Go away."

"No, Pietro." The old woman did not use his new name.

Again she said, "gold," this time whispering it as she swept the coins into her hand, her eyes remaining on Pastore di Capre. Carlo had the glass of grappa to his face and did not hear her last few words.

"This will bring black luck upon you and your family, Pietro." The old woman's voice was just above a whisper. "Your wife is with child again, is she not? You have cursed it with this golden theft. But I can help you." She came very close to his face, "Give me the gold and I will take the curse from it." She narrowed her eyes. "The black luck, it will follow you, Pietro. It will—" but she wasn't able to finish. Pastore di Capre gave her a shove so hard that she landed against the next table.

The crashing of wood caught the tavern owner's attention as he stood behind the bar at the other end of his tavern.

"Stop bothering my patrons!" Chair yelled as the old woman pulled herself upright and shuffled toward the door, sliding the coins into the top of her dress just as the back of her head was struck with enough force to snap it forward. A glass ashtray fell to her feet unbroken. She lifted her hand to the place on her head where she felt wet stickiness inside her hair. As she opened the door, she turned back briefly to see Pastore di Capre standing, another ashtray in his hand.

"Black luck!" she screamed as the second ashtray hit the door, this time shattering onto the floor and the old hag disappeared out into the darkness.

"Take it easy, Pastore," Carlo said. "She's an old gypsy. Why are you getting so upset?"

"Didn't you hear her? She saw the gold—in my hand, the gold."

"No." Carlo emptied his glass as Chair made his way toward the men with two more glasses of grappa. "She says the same thing to everyone." Carlo continued. "She doesn't know." His words dripped carelessly from his mouth like soup.

Chair had arrived at their table and was putting the two new glasses of grappa down. "On me, boys. Sorry about that. I didn't see her come in."

Pastore di Capre felt a panic rise in his chest. He wanted to go home to see Giovanna.

"No thanks. I'm done."

"What? We just sat down," Carlo said. "You didn't even drink yours and look at me?" He pointed to two empty glasses before him as Chair swept them away and replaced them with two full glasses.

"You stay," Pastore di Capre said. He was still standing. He picked up a glass and took a sip. "I'll see you at the house."

"I'll get something to eat here," Carlo answered, "and I'll see you tomorrow morning." He wasn't going to let the grappa go to waste.

Giovanna was delighted to see Pastore di Capre come into the house alone. She looked briefly past him but Pastore di Capre held out his hands. "It's just me."

He pulled her to him, kissing the top of her head, flooded with relief at her flushed face and sparkling eyes — a sure sign of health he thought.

But it was only the next morning that he knew he'd been mistaken, when he awoke to Giovanna's gasp.

"No," she whispered and he knew. He didn't need to see the spots of blood on the sheets as he heard her run into the bathroom.

"Give it to me and I will take the curse from it." The gypsy's words rang in his ears. He had to find her, to remove the black luck, but first he had to climb to the goat shed and retrieve the gold. He thought the old hag would be easy to find. She lived in a hut

outside the village so he decided that he'd stop there on his way up to the pasture to tell her his plan. He was silently mapping it out in his head as Giovanna emerged from the bathroom, wet lines running from her eyes. Pastore di Capre embraced her.

"There will be more. We will try again."

This time he was sure when he said it. He knew the black luck would end as soon as he delivered the gold to the gypsy. He began to pull the soiled sheets from the bed and Giovanna went around to the other side and joined him.

"Do you need the midwife?" Pastore di Capre asked.

"Not this time," Giovanna whispered, her voice trembling ever so slightly.

"Your mother?"

Giovanna shook her head and began to pull the sheet off the bed.

An unexpected series of church bells began to toll, slow and deep. Bong. Bong. Bong. Giovanna looked at the open window and then at Pastore di Capre.

"Who is it? I wonder," she said.

The irony of the death knell did not go unnoticed as they gathered another lost child into the sheets.

Pastore di Capre shrugged his shoulders.

When he met Carlo at the church to begin the ascent to the goat shed, he told him they needed to stop briefly at the gypsy's hut. He wasn't sure how he was going to explain to Carlo his plan to give her the gold—Carlo's gold. But Carlo's response quickly put a stop to the lie Pastore di Capre had started to fabricate.

"The gypsy's dead." Carlo said matter-of-factly, "didn't you hear the bells toll this morning?" He raised his thumb to the silent church tower behind him.

"I did, but I—uh, oh God."

Carlo understood Pastore di Capre's surprise at the news but his distress was unexpected. Of course the ashtray he'd thrown the night before was something several people in the village were thinking about that morning when the news of the old woman's death circulated, but both men knew no one in the tavern would mention it. The old gypsy was no more than a dog or an insect. Would anyone question a kick to a bothersome mutt?

Pastore di Capre needed to stop walking to catch his breath.

"Carlo," he said, "Giovanna lost the baby this morning."

"Ah, I'm sorry, friend." Now, he understood the distress.

"No—you don't understand—the black luck." Pastore di Capre grabbed Carlo's arm, "The gold, Carlo—we stole it. It brought black luck." Carlo was slowly shaking his head, watching his friend carefully as Pastore di Capre continued, his grip a bit tighter, "We have to get rid of it. Throw it into the sea."

Now Carlo was shaking his head with vigor.

"No! We didn't steal it. It's mine. It belongs to the son before the daughters. I'm the son. It's mine." Carlo's words came with a spray of spittle. He felt the emotion in them and quickly reigned it in.

"Pietro—get yourself together. You are upset about the baby. That is understandable. Let me take care of the goats today. I don't need your help. Go home to Gi—"

"Black luck, Carlo! There is no way to kill it." Pastore di Capre now grabbed Carlo's other arm. The two men were face to face. The passersby pretended not to hear the exchange but Carlo saw them watching as Pastore di Capre continued, "the gold, the gold—it's cursed."

"Okay!" Carlo said it quickly and pulled his arms from Pastore di Capre's grip. "Yes, you're right." He lowered his voice. "We have to rid ourselves of it. I'll do it. You go home to Giovanna."

Pastore di Capre was overcome with grief, but not to the degree that he couldn't see through Carlo's lie. He took a deep breath and opened his mouth to speak. He hesitated. "No, I'm okay. I'll come up there with you. You'll need my help to dig."

"The shovel," Carlo said slowly, "I didn't tell you—I broke the handle." He stopped and looked at the ground as if he were searching for something, "I forgot all about it. We need a new one. You, uh—maybe you could go get the one in your yard." Still searching on the ground, he seemed to find what he was looking for and suddenly looked up at Pastore di Capre. "I'll wait at the tavern for you."

"I saw the shovel," Pastore di Capre said, "it's in the goat shed—it's not broken."

"No, you're mistaken. When did you see it? Oh—yes, I put the handle back together but it's going to snap with the slightest pressure. We need yours. Go get it."

Pastore di Capre had known it would be difficult to convince his friend to rid himself of the gold he protected so fervently, so he knew Carlo was weaving some kind of plan—probably to get to the gold first. But it's true—they *would* need a shovel. Pastore di Capre took one step away and then turned back to Carlo.

"We'll ask Chair for a shovel. He's sure to have one."

But if Chair did have one, they wouldn't know for the tavern was closed up tight. It was early in the morning. So Pastore di Capre finally relented and said, "Okay, come with me."

Carlo chuckled half-heartedly, "What? You can't carry a shovel?" He sat down on a large stone outside of the tavern. "I'll wait here. I don't want to disturb Giovanna in her—um, you know—her condition."

He was right about that. Pastore di Capre turned and walked back to the house. And even though Carlo had run all the way to the goat shed the moment Pastore di Capre turned away, it didn't matter, for Pastore di Capre found Giovanna weeping alone in the garden, bent forward over her zinnias. He couldn't leave her—not immediately and so he'd have to trust Carlo.

But he did not.

And with good reason. Carlo had the floor of the goat shed dug up within the hour and the gold coins safely within the cave, deep inside a ravine of which it took him more than an hour to find— with a hole suitable for the pouch of gold coins and then a rock to fit over the hole.

By the time Pastore di Capre returned, Carlo had the goats in the pasture and explained his own muddy tangled appearance by the dug up goat shed floor and his description of his hike to the other side of the ridge to throw the coins into the sea.

It was that day, the moment the lie escaped Carlo's mouth that the two men ceased to be loyal friends. Pastore di Capre remained distrustful until Giovanna's belly grew beyond the term in which she'd previously lost the other babies, grew to full term and then Giovanna called for the midwife. It was then that Pastore di Capre had a brief bout of guilt for doubting his good friend and he vowed to make it right. But Pastore di Capre's son was born days later after an agonizing labor that tore Giovanna to pieces. The tiny boy was as blue as the sea, the umbilical cord wrapped tightly around his throat and that was when Pastore di Capre knew his distrust had been warranted, knew that there'd be only one way to protect his future.

As it happened, Carlo had been watching Pastore di Capre and Giovanna with a sense of what one might call envy, though he himself called admiration. He'd mentioned to Pastore di Capre several times about his sister and the possibility of a match, but Pastore di Capre wouldn't have it. He didn't want Carlo, tainted as he was with the black luck, to infiltrate further into the family. Carlo, on the other hand, eventually gave up on Pastore di Capre's sister and while Giovanna fought the fight of child labor, he negotiated at the tavern with Chair for the hand of his cousin. Chair liked Carlo well enough—though he thought the man drank a bit too much—but his cousin was widowed and a bit older and well she couldn't be picky at her age. Carlo had even mentioned a few gold coins as payment for the arrangement.

When the villagers heard of Pastore di Capre and Giovanna's loss, they attended the funeral, heartbroken as the tiny casket was laid to rest in its grave. They waited the allotted time after the black cloth was taken down from the windows and then made their way to the house to bring food and comfort.

Early one morning, before opening the tavern, Chair and his wife brought a bottle of grappa and fresh beans in tomato sauce. Giovanna's mother took the dish into the kitchen and then led Chair's wife into the bedroom where Giovanna sat in a small wooden rocking chair and looked out the window.

The men went into the yard to smoke and to distance themselves from the solemn whispers that came from the bedroom. Chair wasn't sure how to fill the time with conversation so he discussed the tavern, the weather and then finally Carlo's proposition.

"My cousin, Nina, is going to marry your friend Carlo. I suppose he told you about it."

"He mentioned something," Pastore di Capre lied. "Nina is agreeable to it?"

"Well, at first she wasn't happy at the thought of marrying an outsider. She feared he might want to take her off the island." Chair leaned against the garden wall and took a pack of cigarettes from his pocket. "Carlo assured me he had no such intensions."

Chair took a cigarette from the pack and offered it to Pastore di Capre. Pastore shook his head so Chair put the cigarette in his own mouth. "He's a man of his word, don't you think? Carlo is?" The cigarette was wagging up and down still unlit. Chair shoved his hand into another pocket and pulled out a lighter, a gold coin was sandwiched between the lighter and his fingers. He noticed Pastore di Capre's eyes widen and he looked from the gold coin back to Pastore di Capre. No one carried gold coins anymore.

"From Carlo. Four gold coins for the promise of my cousin." He chuckled half-heartedly. "Archaic, right? But he insisted."

Pastore di Capre felt for the garden wall and leaned next to Chair as Chair lit the cigarette and returned the lighter and gold coin to his pocket.

Pastore di Capre swallowed hard. His son—his first born— dead because of Carlo. Where were the rest of the coins?

"Yes, Carlo is a man of his word." Pastore di Capre's voice was barely a whisper. He stared at the ground for a few moments as Chair sucked at his cigarette. "When is the wedding?"

"Oh, that's not clear yet. Nina just agreed to it yesterday. We need an engagement—a blessing from Father Marco—you know, the whole drawn out way. She wants it all. Maybe it gives her time to really think about it. She insisted on meeting him, a few dinners at the tavern. She's not a young girl anymore. She knows what she's getting into. Maybe she'll back out after some time."

"So, it's not quite decided?"

"I wouldn't say that." Chair worried about what Pastore di Capre would say to his friend. "She looks like she's interested. She said, 'yes' after all. It's just, well—you know—it's not an easy decision. She's a few years older than he—she has the children to think of."

"Yes, the children." Pastore di Capre repeated it slowly.

Chair regretted saying it.

"Chair, I think the payment of gold was correct. Nina is from the old ways and she's right. Carlo might want to return to his village some day." Pastore di Capre knew there was no chance of that. "Four coins are not enough."

Chair's eyebrows went up faster than he could speak, "They're not?" This was not at all what he'd expected. "But the old way would have us paying him, no?"

"No, not with a foreigner such as he is." Pastore di Capre knew Chair would not question the logic, as it had never been tested. "You should have come to me. I could have helped you negotiate." Pastore di Capre continued. "He cheated you. After all, Nina has the house and the fishing boat. And you know, he did tell me he was tired of the goats. And you Chair—you have the tavern. He'd be family and you know how he drinks. He has everything to gain from this arrangement. He cheated you."

So Pastore di Capre was not as loyal to his friend as was surmised by the villagers.

"You think so?" Now Chair felt foolish. "I couldn't come to you. Giovanna was, uh, well you know. It didn't seem right and when Carlo suggested I leave you out of it, I had to agree. You and Giovanna were—" He didn't know how to finish but he suddenly saw Carlo's deceit. Carlo had kept Pastore di Capre out of the deal so he could keep his gold! Chair realized he'd been cheated. Now it was clear.

"We've already agreed to the deal. There's nothing I can do."

Chair was sick at the thought of negotiating this union, allowing this outsider into his family—someone even Pastore di Capre, who knew him better than anyone on the island, had not let his own sister marry. What a fool he had been.

"We shook on it."

"But you, yourself, said that Nina might change her mind, no?"

"Yes." Chair said it slowly and looked up at Pastore di Capre.

"Tell him today," Pastore di Capre said. "Go find him before he goes up to the pasture. You want four more."

"It seems wrong. Greedy."

"This is Nina you're talking about. If she doesn't go through with it, you can return them. If she does—well, make it a wedding gift to her. Either way, you'll be free of guilt. But the higher price makes it more, let's say—equitable. And then you can see if his intensions are honorable."

Chair was silent. He was looking into the distance as if looking for a hint of the future. "Hm. I don't know."

"Does he want a wife?" Pastore di Capre said with strength, "or does he want a house, a boat, your tavern!"

That was enough. The tavern—Pastore di Capre found the soft spot in Chair's integrity.

"Go now, before he goes to the pasture." Pastore di Capre pushed a bit further, "before you lose your nerve. Your wife will be here when you return. Go."

"The pasture?"

"No—the fruit seller's apartment. He'll just be leaving now.

Why should you climb to the pasture? You have better things to do than run after him. Go."

It was only a few minutes later that Chair returned triumphant, a smile on his face as he entered Pastore di Capre's living room.

And it was only moments after, that Pastore di Capre set off to find Carlo on the mountain but when he reached the pasture only the goats were there and when he peeked into the goat shed, the shovel was leaning in it's usual place. So he continued his climb to where the castle sat beside the cave.

Pastore di Capre was making his way over the fallen rocks of the castle's façade when he heard an almost inaudible sound from within the cave and he changed direction.

Inside the cave, his eyes adjusted to the dark almost immediately. He guided himself along the wall, feeling the rough edges with his hand, his feet testing each step before placing his foot down. Step by step, with the silence of a prowling animal, he made his way to the deep crevice against the far wall. He knew it well.

This was *his* cave. All of it—the boulders that lay side by side where they'd fallen from the ceiling after seismic shakes of the island, and the cool wet surface as he knelt at the edge of the crevice and saw the beam of Carlo's flashlight and the top of his head. Pastore di Capre's breath came slowly against the cave air, his mouth slightly open and his eyes wide as he watched Carlo from above. He was but an appendage of the stones, a droplet of mist in the cool air—invisible to an unsuspecting Carlo as Carlo carefully opened the small burlap bag of gold, retrieved a few coins and then drew the string tightly around the pouch and bent to return it to the hole. Carlo had not yet slid the rock over the hiding place when he froze. His head turned slightly as his ears searched for understanding. As he looked up, he had only milliseconds to understand as a rock, as large as his head, smashed into his face, pushing the cartilage of his nose far back into his brain and the flashlight rolled into the hole with the gold.

Pastore di Capre's limbs barely felt the side of the crevice as he followed behind the giant rock he'd kicked over the side. The slight groan that escaped Carlo's mouth caused Pastore di Capre to pick up another rock and smash it once, twice—how many times, he wasn't quite sure—for he saw the lifeless blue body of his son, there in the darkness. The sound of rock against breaking skull bones continued until that image washed away.

It was that motion of his hand, pulling up and smashing downward again and again, the sound of crushing bone like broken seashells in a bag, and that small groan that had escaped the crevice into the cave's dank dark world that would forever remain in Pastore di Capre's memory while all else slowly flowed away like water through a storm drain. Those remnants invaded his dreams, his thought and now, fifty-something years later his whole life. The only memory stronger was that of the gypsy's words—*black luck has fallen upon you and your family. It will follow you.* Without her incantations, he was never sure if the curse had been lifted.

Now—as he wandered in and out of time—only Carlo and the gypsy stayed constant—always there to torment him. Even if he could not find Giovanna or his house or his lifelong friends, even if he was unsure of what day or season or year it was, even if the voices that came from unfamiliar faces had a familiar ring—Carlo was always there, his voice booming with drunken laughter, his back bending over the milking pail, and his burlap pouch as it sailed from Pastore di Capre's hands over the cliff and among the rocks of the sea at the far end of the island. And Pastore di Capre was never sure. Was it gone? Had he destroyed the black luck?

His uncertainty after Chair had come to help him remove the body was eventually washed away with the birth of his daughter, Angelina, shortly after Carlo's one-year memorial. Carlo had been laid to rest in the village cemetery and had all the rituals any villager would have had, for the man had lived among them for over two whole years. The villagers accepted Carlo's death, a terrible accident on the ridge with the goats. He was a foreigner after all and most likely did not realize the dangers of walking among the loose rocks of a cliff.

No, Pastore di Capre never regretted his actions as he watched his daughter grow and prosper. It wasn't until his grandson's arrest, when Rocco, just a fifteen-year-old child was sent away for a full ten years, a punishment for a murder that no doubt belonged to Pastore di Capre. The sins of the grandfather visited upon the sons of the future. Then, the uncertainty came back and haunted his thoughts. He worried relentlessly for what lay ahead.

Now, as Pastore di Capre's mind slowly turned to blank paper, Carlo ceased to inhabit his dreams and daily thoughts. No, instead Carlo walked among the villagers on the other side of the garden wall and Carlo visited Pastore di Capre regularly—coming to his house, talking to his wife, ascending the mountain to milk the goats and then to sit in the tavern. Day after day, he sat at a dark table in the corner of the tavern with one companion—the gypsy woman—patiently waiting for Pastore di Capre.

CHAPTER 9

Rocco sat on the bottom step of the apartment stairs at the back of the pizzeria, his feet flat on the floor, his head resting on his knees, his torso a heavy mass of boneless gel. The black sky was barely visible through the torrents of rain that fell like solid sheets of silver and hammered against the open door and down onto the pavement outside. It was just after midnight. Everyone was asleep — except Rocco.

The back door was propped open with the broken toolbox that he'd put in place before he'd rolled the K-2 into the cigarette paper. The rain flooded the parking lot and pushed a small stream of water along the building and past the door frame. The *cigarette* smoke was just dissipating. Rocco watched the empty silver packet as the wind picked it up violently and spun it in rapid arches over the cluttered tile floor of the vestibule and then slammed it down onto the wet floor.

His eyes stared, unblinking, his mouth hung open and his breath came in short slow skips. A heavy gust slid under the K-2 packet. It rose from the floor again, this time a little higher and then — bam — straight down onto the toolbox that was now wet and muddy. Rocco blinked but was unable to look away. Again the wind grabbed the silver packet. Straight up again, looping in the air and then down hard, just at the door's edge near two small bare feet. The feet were as wet as the door that dripped with long lines of rainwater and the toenails at the end of those wet feet had lines of pink and blue on them. The toes came into the vestibule, stopping in front of Rocco. He tried to look up, but his head was glued to his knees and his neck no longer connected to his spine.

Two hands came down and held each side of his face. Slowly the hands turned his head, first back and forth to loosen it from his knees and then up and down. Yes—he understood. This is how his neck should work.

The figure lowered itself to the floor so that it sat directly in front of him. It was a woman—maybe—but he wasn't sure. Her skin, translucent, shone like the glow of an ember under her wet clothes. It was skin that he wanted to touch. He reached out and stroked her wet face and then her neck, his fingers pulsing against a rhythm, like a heartbeat. Her eyes were glass, her lips dark blue. He felt her breath on his face. It was as hot as the steam from the open pizza oven. He could feel it cover him and heat him to an almost unbearable degree. He slid his hand down the curve of her neck and felt the smoothness of her shoulder. She smiled and he felt an unconditional razor-sharp love. It lingered and settled over them like a finely woven net. As his hand slid along the pink arm, she reached for it and his fingers began to melt. He was becoming part of her, his hand disappearing into the fabric of her wet skin. And she pulled him from the stairs until he lay on top of her and she lay with her back on the wet floor. He began to sink into her body. Slowly his legs melding to hers and then a gust of wind sent a jet of air beneath the two of them. They were lifted as easily as the empty silver packet. Rocco's head melted into the crook of her neck as the wind pulled them out into the rain and up above the dark branches along the fence.

The thunder caused Angelina to toss and turn but her exhausted body stayed just beyond wakefulness. Patrice slid from the bed and walked from the room to use the bathroom. She tiptoed past her father on the sofa, but he had been awakened by the storm also. The telephone's digital screen glowed green on the coffee table, five o' clock, and the sky shone gray in the window.

"Sorry," Patrice whispered, "did I wake you?"

He shook his head and pulled the blanket higher around his chin. "The storm," he said.

Patrice nodded and continued to the bathroom but saw Rocco's bedroom door open and peeked in there first. He wasn't there. She decided to go to the refrigerator under the hot plate to get a drink of juice. She opened the refrigerator and bent to look inside. It was empty. She straightened up and stood on her toes to look out the window.

Pasquale whispered to her. "Are you using the bathroom or not?"

"Yes," she said. The car was still in its parking place beside the dumpster. Where could he be? "I mean, no," Patrice said to her father, "You go first."

As her father disappeared into the bathroom, she opened the apartment door that led to the stairs and flicked on the light. At first she didn't see him, as the flooded floor and open door had caught her eye. But as she rushed down the stairs, a soggy lump on the floor moved and Patrice stopped dead on the bottom stair and gave a little yelp.

Rocco lay in nothing but boxer shorts, a curled up ball at the foot of the stairs. The side of his face that had been submerged in a puddle of water remained wrinkled and red as he brought his head upright and looked at his sister.

"Patrice."

He said her name but nothing else. He seemed to be noticing his surroundings for the first time and quickly pulled the toolbox from the door causing it to snap shut.

"Damn," he whispered.

Patrice stood with her hand on the banister and her eyes wide. "What are you—" She didn't quite finish her question as her voice trailed off. She watched him stand, his lips blue and shivering. He held the wall for a moment, steadying himself.

"Damn, Patrice." It was just above a whisper and his lips curved into a smile. "It was great."

His foot was on the bottom step and Patrice pushed to the side to let him pass. Her brows were pulled together as she watched Rocco's feet leave mud and leaves on each step as he ascended.

"Great?" She was confused.

He didn't answer.

Pasquale was standing at the top of the stairs.

"What's happening here? A leak? From where?"

He was half way down the stairs and pushing past Rocco before he noticed how wet his son was.

"Are you crazy? Going out in just boxers. You'll catch your death." Pasquale was at the bottom of the stairs. "Look at this mess." He looked back up at his children. Rocco was at the top of the stairs. Patrice continued to hold the railing and look from her father to her brother.

"Sorry," Rocco said. He couldn't steady his body as he shivered uncontrollably. "I thought I heard someone out there. I went to check and I uh, slipped in the rain."

"What?" Pasquale was shaking his head, looking down at the puddle in the vestibule. It had bits of paper and leaves floating in it. He looked back up at his son but Rocco had disappeared into the apartment. He looked at Patrice who only shrugged her shoulders and gave him a look of solidarity.

A few days went by before Patrice agreed to contact Josh. She didn't tell Rocco that she and Josh texted a couple hundred times a day. That's how she found out about the K-2. Eventually, though with Josh's visits to the store and with conversations through Patrice, Rocco learned that those little packets were legal, cheap and sold at a bodega in the next town, just a few exits north on the highway. So when the timing belt in Pasquale's car broke, and Josh offered to fix it, Rocco volunteered to accompany Josh to the auto parts store which just happened to be a few exits north on the highway.

*   *   *   *

Josh was standing at the front of the car that was parked near the dumpster behind the pizzeria. The car hood was propped open. Patrice was sitting in the driver's seat with her feet on the pavement outside the car. The motor hummed lightly. Josh looked up pushed the car hood down and it slammed shut.

"Sounds good. You can turn it off now."

He was just coming around to the car door as Patrice twisted her body and leaned toward the steering wheel. The engine died as she pulled the key from the ignition and looked up at Josh with awe. With nothing but a few tools and pieces of thin rubber, he had changed water to wine, spun straw to gold, and slain the evil dragon. He had fixed the car and won the trust of her parents.

Josh sensed the victory as Patrice reached for his greasy hands and pulled him toward her. He bent and kissed her on the mouth. A long warm kiss with her full soft lips pressed against his — much more satisfying than a text message with emojis.

That was the day that Josh was welcomed through the back door of the store, the day his dirty hands in the kitchen sink drew smiles from Angelina, the day Pasquale hugged him and said a broken English thank you. And he enjoyed that new status tremendously. It was one that brought him into the bosom of their family, a family of which he longed to be a member. And it brought him closer to the girl he intended to marry some day.

"You bring mother, father," Pasquale said but then turned to Angelina for help. "Tell him to invite his parents to the store. We'll cook them something."

"Okay," Angelina shooed Pasquale from the kitchen. "Go help Javier out there." She looked at Patrice, "Javier's daughter is sweet, but she doesn't quite get the computer. Go back out there with Papa."

Patrice looked from her mother to Josh and hesitated.

"I'm not going to bite him," she said in English and smiled at Josh. "Don't worry. Go."

"I'll be out in a second." Josh said as he pulled his hands from the water and Angelina handed him a towel.

"Where do you live, Josh?" Her eyes narrowed. She wasn't going to give in to her daughter's pleas quite yet. "In Robin's Nest?"

"Uh, no—just two exits up. Brownsville. You know where the dealership is? A few miles from there, near the hospital."

This piqued her suspicion, his not being from the same village. It was hard to change the mindset she'd brought over from Incompresso. She'd have to grill Patrice a bit more on how they'd met, but she wondered about the family he came from.

"What does your father do?"

Josh swallowed hard. His hands were dry and he wanted very much to go into the pizzeria and be with Patrice. "He's um, I think he's a—he drives a truck." He wanted to lie, but he knew it would hurt his chance more than the information about his father. "I haven't seen him since I was a little kid."

"I see."

"No—you don't," Josh thought, *"I'm not him."*

He quickly said, "My mother is an accountant." Maybe Patrice's mother didn't know what that was. "She keeps the books at Spencer's, the sports store, um and she does taxes and stuff like that."

"I know what an accountant is." Angelina's voice had lost its softness.

"I have an older sister. She's married. Her husband, uh, he, um, you know—he is a really good guy. He takes care of his family and they've been married a long time."

Five years wasn't exactly a long time but he somehow wanted to negate his father's absence. "He and I are really close." Somewhat true, though it's hard to be close to someone who lives twelve hours away.

"Hm. Well, we'd like to invite your family to a meal here. Do you think they'd like that?"

Oh no.

"Ah—well my sister and her husband don't live near by and well he works a lot." Josh drew the last few words out for emphasis. "But my mother, yeah. She'll come." The invitation felt like one more victory.

When Josh told his mother, she was less than enthusiastic.

"It's my busy season, Josh." She was just coming into the house. It was dark and later than usual. "Who are these people anyway?"

Josh followed her around the house as she threw her sweater over a kitchen chair and then headed for the office next to the dining room. She threw her briefcase on the desk and was half-listening as Josh went through the monologue of how he'd met Patrice and the significance of the dinner invitation and how he'd appreciate her coming. And when was she available? He continued following her, keeping pace with her stride as she went back to the kitchen. Again he asked her when she thought she might be available.

"Huh?" His mother had the refrigerator open and a piece of cold chicken in her mouth. "Available? You're serious?" She was chewing as she talked and she put the chicken down on the counter as she grabbed a bottle of water and closed the refrigerator.

"How about Tuesday?" Josh asked. It was his day off.

His mother took a long drink of water. "Not possible." She popped the rest of the chicken in her mouth and said, "not at all this month."

"You can come from work. Just eat something and excuse yourself."

She was headed back to her home-office near the dining room. She stopped and looked at Josh—still chewing. "Excuse myself?"

"I'll tell them you're coming from work. You eat a few bites and say you've gotta go."

"What happened to that other one? What was her name? Ashley?"

Josh was losing his patience, "Ma—come on. What's your point? You can't just take an hour or two for me?"

Oh there it was, that ungrateful little twerp.

"Who do you think I've been doing this for, all these years?" The storm clouds rolled in and circled around her head.

"Okay. Okay." Josh knew it was too late. He waited for the tirade.

"Do you see anyone else here paying the bills? Who do you think has kept this roof over your head?" Her voice grew louder. "And a nice one too, a good neighborhood, a good school. How the hell do you think it happened all these years? The money fairy?"

Josh sighed. *"I didn't ask for it,"* he thought. *"Just having someone around would have been nice."* But Josh was a smart person. He wasn't going to blow his chances with Patrice. "You're right, ma."

"Damn right—I'm right! And now I'm going to continue providing. That's right—providing more and more and more." She was closing the office door between them. "What else do you want from me? You want blood?" The door was closed and Josh walked away.

Angelina and Pasquale paid taxes on their store, plenty of them. They had an accountant who came to the apartment in tax season so they understood Josh's request to wait a while for the *family* dinner. Angelina told Josh that the summer might be a better time for them also. She was thinking of the new house she hoped they'd have by then. Maybe there'd even be a dining room.

She was assembling pizza boxes at the back of the store as Josh left. It was a very monotonous task and allowed her a few minutes of daydreaming. She pictured the house that she wanted. She'd talked to the relator a few times, so she had a good image in her mind and now that the lawyer had confirmed Javier's ability to become a partner, she thought about it more often.

It would take some time. That suited her just fine. It gave her a chance to see Rocco take control and a chance to bring her parents over to get the care they needed. Robin's Nest wasn't far from the hospital. It was only two exits to the north on the highway and it was one of the best. That's what Patrice had said when she searched for information on her telephone. Big Antonio had explained what the doctor at the medical center had said when he helped Giovanna there after she'd fallen on the path between their homes. Her ankle was only sprained but the doctor had recognized the shaking in her limb as he tried to wrap it. And he'd asked how she was coping with her husband's dementia. The young doctor had recommended a type of therapy but that was on the mainland. Those were some of the things Big Antonio told Angelina when he betrayed Giovanna's trust with another phone call.

Angelina thought an American hospital could surely fix whatever ailment her two old parents had. She thought of the house that they'd buy to make the two as comfortable as possible but to also alleviate her own guilt. And in the end—just as the lawyer had told them—they'd be able to sell the house and make a profit. They'd be able to go back. By then, Rocco would surely have found a nice girl from a good family. He might even be able to buy his own house. Maybe the girl's family owned property somewhere. It wasn't so far fetched a dream. She suspected his recent trips alone in the evenings had something to do with a girl. He looked a little trimmer, as though he were taking more care of his appearance, though a bit haggard. What else could it be? No doubt he was taking his cue from his sister for she surely was happier now that Josh was in the pizzeria more frequently.

Patrice and Josh—maybe their relationship could be a marriage with grandchildren. Then she and Pasquale would be able to travel between Incompresso and America. She longed for the comfort of her birthplace while pining for the newness of other places. Maybe she'd be able to get to England after all. Who knows how much of a profit they'd make from the house that they'd yet to buy.

Her thoughts turned back to her parents, to their sudden fragility and the sense that she was looking at her own future with Pasquale. And time was slowly ticking away.

A hand on her shoulder woke her from her reverie. It was Patrice holding out her cell phone.

"Mama, it's Big Antonio again," Patrice said.

*   *   *   *

In Pastore di Capre's condition, the trip from Incompresso to Robin's Nest would be a tricky one. The plan was for Big Antonio to help Angelina get them to the airport, first on the ferry and then in the taxi. After Big Antonio's telephone call about her mother's fall, so soon after her ankle injury, Angelina awoke to the reality of the situation and she knew it couldn't wait one day more. She couldn't wait for the purchase of the new house.

She had arrived on Incompresso a few days before and without much rest was prepared to return to Robin's Nest with her parents. Big Antonio's son, Little Antonio, had left his fishing boat for the day and would also be coming to help them as far as the airport, though he hadn't yet arrived at the house. At the airport, Angelina had arranged for two wheelchairs.

"I'm not an invalid, Angelina," Giovanna had said when her daughter told her the plan. "Not yet, anyway."

"I know that, Mama. It just makes it easier. The airport is big and with two people in wheelchairs, I'll be able to get help from the people there."

It was a terrible turn of the tide, having one's child become the caregiver and having to submit to those decisions. Giovanna tried to picture herself in a wheelchair being pushed around but all she could conjure up was a baby carriage.

Angelina was standing in front of the living room window trying to close the shutters, pulling them inward and trying to latch them, but the hinges were not cooperating. The shutters hadn't been closed since the hurricane-like winds blew through, many years before, so Maria was outside pushing them while Angelina pulled.

Anna Maria and her daughter Anna were also there. They'd brought an orange, picked moments before from an orange tree in their yard. It didn't matter that it wasn't anywhere near ripe or edible. Giovanna needed something from Incompresso, something that had grown there and carried seeds – to ensure a safe passage and good luck in her new home. So they had their orange, rock hard and barely the color of its name. They gave it to Giovanna who put it in her purse where it would stay the entire trip. Angelina watched her mother kiss them on both cheeks and thank them, tears rolling down the faces of all three.

"I thought you'd be able to see my baby. She's due next month," Anna said.

They'd become closer since Anna was part of the brigade that Father Marco had put together. Her designated day was Tuesday, right after her visit to the medical center and before she headed to the preschool to help the cook in the kitchen. She usually spent her two hours helping Giovanna clean the house or just sitting with Pastore di Capre so Giovanna could simply feel the caregiver yoke lifted for a while.

"I'll be back soon," Giovanna, said, "I'll be at the christening, you'll see." She brushed some hair away from Anna's face. "And with that fancy American medicine, I'll even be dancing!" She laughed.

Angelina knew the fancy-American comment, was for her benefit. It had taken all of her effort to convince her mother to leave the island. And it wasn't until she told Giovanna that Pastore di Capre might be able to get treatment and maybe communicate with them again, that Giovanna relented.

Angelina wasn't exactly sure how that would happen but it's what she'd read online in Patrice's telephone after Gina had shown up at the pizzeria with her husband. It was the exact moment after Angelina had spoken to Big Antonio and heard the new update of her parents' condition. He'd told her about her mother falling again and this time hurting her wrist—an ankle and wrist injury—not good. With that new information coupled with the story Big Antonio had told her about her mother becoming *frozen* in front of the oven, Angelina could no longer ignore the inevitable.

After listening to Big Antonio on Patrice's telephone, Angelina had not been able to make it back to the kitchen before the tears erupted. It was actually Gina's husband who had helped her as she swayed and the walls of the pizzeria began to spin. She hadn't know it was him until Gina was at his side but Angelina didn't want to think about the husband, especially how kind and gentle he was when she'd been wishing him dead for so long. Yet there he was grabbing her before she went to the floor—Gina behind him with eyes that dripped with guilt and repentance. Angelina had seen the expression on Rocco's face just before Gina's husband stepped into view and her heart was torn in two. No, not now—she couldn't think of her son when she had such a weight to carry right here, on Incompresso.

Angelina gave the old house one more thorough look to see if she'd forgotten anything. Chair was in the yard talking to Big Antonio. He'd helped bring the suitcases out—four of them—and was going to help Big Antonio and his son bring them to the ferry. He stuck his head inside the front door.

"Did you turn off the water and electricity?"

The look on Angelina's face told him the answer. "I didn't even think of it," she said. "That's something Papa would have done immediately." She sighed and looked at her father on the sofa who looked at Chair as he approached.

Pastore di Capre raised his hand in a greeting.

"How about a drink?"

"Come by the tavern sometime," Chair answered as he passed.

"That's a good idea. I will."

Chair disappeared into the kitchen and Angelina heard him fiddling around with the water lever behind the sink. He came out and looked at her, nodded his head and then disappeared into the bathroom. More tinkering noises and then he reappeared at the fuse panel in the hallway near the living room.

"Are you ready? It's going to get very dark. Take him outside."

"Am I ready?" Angelina thought. *"Ready to uproot these people who know nothing else. Ready to plant them in a country that is as foreign to them as the moon? Ready to take on this burden that has as great a weight as the new house and the split profits of the pizzeria? No, I'm not ready – not at all!"*

"I'm ready," Angelina said quietly as she helped her father stand and shooed the three other women from the house.

As Big Antonio held the garden gate open, Giovanna hesitated. She looked back at the house. Was she a bird leaving her cage or one captured and forced to leave her habitat? Even to her it was unclear, for the pressure of caring for herself and Pastore di Capre had, at times, felt so pressing, so confining that she longed to have an answer put into her hands. And now that the answer was America, she had to believe it was true. After all, she'd be with her daughter and with her grandchildren—and yes, Pasquale— though it was hard not to blame him for taking them all away. The fool could have continued his very fine life with the goats, here on Incompresso.

"Wait," Giovanna said. "I don't know your telephone number." She was looking at Big Antonio. "What if I want to call you?"

He and Maria hadn't thought of that either. He quickly wrote it on a piece of paper that Angelina provided from her purse. Of course she had the telephone number. How else had she been calling her mother from America? But Angelina said nothing. She simply took the paper from Big Antonio.

"I want to hold it," Giovanna said. Somehow it gave her comfort to have what she perceived as a lifeline to the island.

"I'm giving it to you," Angelina answered as she scribbled more numbers on the paper. "You have to add a few numbers to the beginning when you call from the U.S."

She handed the paper to her mother and Giovanna stuffed it into her coat pocket.

"Don't forget about the zinnias," Giovanna said to Maria.

"The zinnias?" Angelina asked as she looked at the dry weeds of her mother's garden.

Big Antonio waved the back of his hand at Angelina, dismissing her confusion and he looked at Giovanna in earnest. "We won't forget. I promise."

Maria nodded her head in agreement.

"Okay, let's go," Angelina said as Little Antonio came around the corner.

"C'mon, the ferry's going to leave soon," Little Antonio said as he took a suitcase from his father and scratched his bald head.

The small group began to move toward the harbor just as the church bells began to chime their unhealthy clang-dink. It was meant only to announce the Sunday service but Giovanna suddenly stopped walking.

"I have to go to the church," she said abruptly. "One last time. I want to light a candle . . . for the trip."

"We'll miss the ferry, Mama."

"I'll hold the ferry," Chair said as he picked up a suitcase, "Come on, Antonio. Let's get going. You too, Angelina. Grab your father. Maria, help Angelina."

Chair waved his hand at Giovanna and looked at Angelina. "Leave your mother to go. It's okay." He nodded at Big Antonio's son. "You, Little Antonio, go ahead and tell the captain we're coming."

"Are you okay alone, Mama?" Angelina asked.

"Of course I'm okay."

Chair looked from one to the other and said, "Yes, yes, she's fine. Go ahead Giovanna." He waved his hand at her and to the rest he said, "let's go. I'll talk to the ferry captain."

Chair remembered the ashtray hitting the back of the gypsy's head and Carlo's bashed in skull. It was no coincidence to him that it was the *head* of Pastore di Capre that had been slowly deteriorating.

"Yes, go to the church, Giovanna," he said.

Why give the dead an opportunity to extract more vengeance?

CHAPTER 10

So it was settled. Javier's daughter was the new partner in the pizzeria, a twenty-year-old American born girl with the brains of an empty canister. She and Pasquale were now co-owners of the business until the lawyer could get the papers set for Javier to take over. In the haste after Big Antonio's telephone call, it seemed the most prudent plan because it produced the immediate down payment for the purchase of a house that was taking so long to finalize.

"Such simple matters seemed to take forever in this place," Pasquale thought as he helped Rocco ready the apartment over the pizzeria.

They moved the bed out of the bedroom and squeezed it next to the sofa. That made enough space inside the bedroom for his in-laws' two twin beds that would be delivered within the hour. Pasquale stood in front of the sofa and looked at the large bed pushed up against it. He was also thinking about the volume and decibel load of his son's snoring. Well, it couldn't be helped. It was just until the closing on the small home behind the pizzeria, and then they'd have an entire house and eventually his in-laws would be in the detached garage he planned on transforming for them.

Now, it was getting late and Pasquale needed to get downstairs. He could hear Javier coming in the back door, below.

Patrice had already gone down to start the pizza ovens. Rocco was going to pick up his mother and grandparents at the airport. He'd have to leave soon if he were to make it there on time. But he thought it would be fine to just make a quick stop, off the exit to the north before heading further up to the airport.

But it wasn't fine.

And Angelina was in a full-blown panic when she finally pulled the telephone from her bag as she stood at the curb where the airline agent had helped her roll the two wheelchairs. The suitcases were piled on the sidewalk next to them. As Angelina dialed the phone, she tried to get her father to stay sitting in his wheelchair by yelling at him, as her patience had dissipated long before the sedative they'd given him.

Yes, Rocco had left hours ago, Patrice told her. Patrice was more annoyed than worried. Just get in a taxi, she told her mother. Yes, it would be expensive but what alternative was there now? No one else could come get her.

Neither Patrice nor Pasquale understood the hardship Angelina had endured trying to keep Pastore di Capre's anxiety to a muted level for the last seven hours and she'd expected Rocco's familiar face to calm him. But where the hell was Rocco and why didn't he answer his telephone?

*   *   *   *   *

Joe was in the emergency room again. They'd called him down to help with the influx of admissions. He texted Gina to let her know about the car accident victims and that he couldn't meet her for lunch. This time she actually responded with an *okay*, which immediately diffused his worry over her slipping back into her gloom. Since his rescue of the pizza woman the other day, he sensed the old Gina making an appearance now and then. At least that's how he saw it.

He'd insisted they stop and eat there together. He wanted to get a better look inside and see what it was that seemed to pull her there every few days. After Lucas' telephone call from his police car, Joe was more alarmed at his wife's behavior. Waiting it out was simply not working. Lucas had called and said he'd stopped Gina. She was behaving oddly and she'd been swerving all over the road, sort of like a drunk driver, but she wasn't drunk. That telephone call had caused Joe to realize he couldn't just sit back and watch her unravel. He needed to be more active in her recovery.

"I doubt that she's drunk," he'd said to his friend. "She's not a drinker and that wouldn't make any sense."

Joe had been looking at the rice on the cold stove as he spoke to Lucas, the television blaring in the background. He'd walked over to it and searched for the power button. He would later find the remote control in Gina's car.

As he'd pressed the power button on the front of the television he'd said to Lucas, "What kind of cop are you, anyway? You let her drive?"

"I said she *acted like*, not that she *was* drunk. I could see she wasn't." Lucas answered. "I'm watching her pull back onto the road right now. I'm not going to follow her or anything. I was just giving you a heads up. She doesn't seem herself."

"Yeah, no kidding." Joe rarely used such sarcasm.

The slices of peperoni on the car door, the soggy pizza box soaking into the front seat of the car and the mess of hardened cheese and sauce on the gear changer all pointed to that darn pizzeria again and he was determined to stop there and see what the attraction was. It's what he had planned to do the following day but then he had worked late and then the day after, his mother-in-law had needed his car so he just never got there. So a few days later, as they rounded the corner on Main Street, it occurred to him that if Gina were with him when he did finally go, he'd be able to see her reaction, to see what exactly it was she did there.

The airline tickets to Italy had not yet been purchased. Joe had been hesitant. He checked the flights often but he hadn't yet been able to commit to a day or a time. Not yet—there remained a barrier between him and his wife—an invisible wall of sorts. Her feelings of grief—those were things he'd been privy to until recently, when suddenly she'd tuned him out. She's just stopped talking. But why? The answer had to be at that pizzeria. Who goes to a pizzeria several times a week? It was in that store—the answer to her baffling behavior—that *something* that seemed to trigger a look of loathing that sliced him in half. Maybe he could diffuse it in some way.

So as they were coming home from her mother's house, driving on Main Street, he'd seen the pizzeria and decided to turn into the parking lot. And he knew he was right because Gina's agitation wasn't at all warranted.

"What are you doing?" she'd said abruptly and louder than intended. The turn was so unexpected, that she hadn't been able to check her emotions before she spoke. She looked quickly at the pizzeria and then at Joe and then at the car door as if she were about to jump out.

"How about some pizza. We can eat here." Joe answered.

"No. I don't want to—I, uh don't feel like it, Joe. We just ate at my mother's."

"That was hours ago. I'm hungry. You don't have to have anything."

"No. I'll stay in the car."

Joe had parked the car and turned the engine off. "Stay in the car? Why? Come and sit inside with me."

"No. I'm tired. Get it *to go*. I'm staying here." Gina's head had been turned away from him and he saw her looking in the side mirror.

"Fine."

He wasn't backing down. He wanted to see inside. What was all the fuss about, a pizza box in the trash a few times a week? It was ridiculous and he was tired of ignoring it and waiting for things to go back to normal.

As he came through the store entrance, a young girl at the register had tried to greet him but she was speaking Italian into a cell phone and was only able to nod in his direction.

"*Typical,*" Joe thought shaking his head as he waited, "*kids with cell phones. Ridiculous.*"

There'd been two men, one older than he and one younger. They looked at each other and then at Joe and then at the window that faced the parking lot where he'd parked Gina's blue sedan.

The young girl had pulled away from the telephone and said, "I'm so sorry. One minute." She'd put her finger up to emphasize the one minute and then walked back to an older woman who was assembling pizza boxes at a table in the back of the store. She'd handed the telephone to the older woman and then came back to the counter.

"How can I help you?"

But Joe had already found his answer. It was uncanny, the resemblance. The older man looked so much like Gina's father, Joe's heart softened and he said, "I'll take a slice of pizza to go, please." And then he nodded his head in greeting at the old guy who was staring at him as though he were an aberration. Joe guessed that the younger man was his son for they looked very much alike. The younger man said something to his father who then said, "hello," and turned his back to Joe. As Joe gave Patrice his debit card, he saw Angelina stumble against the table and the telephone in her hand fell to the floor.

Joe's nursing instinct kicked in and he was at Angelina's side long before Pasquale could get around the counter. The tears streamed from her eyes as she apologized profusely and the entire store seemed to stop all movement—except for Gina running through the door. When she'd seen everyone quickly move away from the front window, she'd imagined a brawl of some kind and had run in, thinking she'd have to help pull Joe and Rocco apart.

In the emergency room now, Joe remembered the incident and tried to stay focused.

"*Yes,*" he thought as he rushed to a gurney near the ambulance entrance. "*That's it. Gina seemed to return to herself after the pizza-woman incident.*"

He grabbed the gurney handles from the EMT, gave him a nod and started pushing it toward the triage room. The EMT followed for a few steps, putting a clipboard on the patient's chest when Joe ignored his extended arm.

"*The old pizza-guy must have reminded her of her father,*" Joe thought. After they'd gotten back in their car and he'd suggested that to her, she seemed to change.

"Whatta we got?" The ER nurse asked Joe as she slid a blood pressure sleeve around the old man's arm and grabbed the clipboard.

This lunch date with Gina was something to which Joe was very much looking forward. He was frustrated at having to cancel. The old man on the gurney was staring up at him. Joe gave himself a mental smack in the head. He had to concentrate.

"What's your name sir?" Joe was looking at the old man. The old man said nothing.

"Unresponsive," Joe said to the other nurse.

"Says here he's hearing impaired," the nurse said as she looked at the clipboard, "You didn't read it? Are there hearing aids somewhere?" She looked more closely at the man's ears.

"Sorry." Joe said, as he left the patient and went back to the ER doors where another victim was being rolled in. A uniformed police officer followed the gurney with some urgency.

"Overdose." The officer said, "He's not with the accident. John Doe. No ID." The young man was unconscious. Joe thought of K-2 but then he saw the needle marks on the patient's arm as he rolled up his sleeve for the blood pressure cuff and then he saw the face. The young man's eyes stared up at Joe and blinked a few times. It was the son from the pizzeria. It was Rocco.

The police officer spoke to Joe as Joe grabbed a stethoscope and listened to Rocco's heart. "He was worse when we found him. Bodega owner called us." He handed Joe a paper. Joe was visibly shaken.

The officer continued, "I administered *Narcan* immediately. Otherwise, we would've lost him."

Rocco was lucky. The Brownsville police had just been given *Narcan* for immediate use to reverse the depressed state of opiates in a person who appeared to no longer be breathing. Had it been a week prior, he'd have been on a gurney in the morgue rather than a bed in the ER.

"Listen, I know this kid," Joe said.

"Really? My partner thought he was an illegal. I think he notified ICE."

"ICE?" Joe was rolling Rocco's arm back and forth, looking for a place to insert the intravenous needle.

"Immigration."

"No. I know him. He's not an illegal."

The triage nurse came over and nodded to the officer.

"I got it Joe." Joe handed her the IV lead. His hands were shaking. "We're good now," she said. She was glad to get rid of him. "It's under control."

"Maybe you could give us a name?" The officer said to Joe.

Joe nodded. "I know him from a—actually, I don't know his name. My wife might. Let me text her."

Gina was sitting in the break room staring at her phone when the text buzzed through.

What's the pizza son's name?

Her stomach churned.

Rocco. Why?

He's down here. Overdose. Last name?

Gina sat staring at the words for a few seconds.

I don't know.

OK. See you tonight.

CHAPTER 11

Giovanna was exhausted as she looked at the mountain of stairs before her. She was standing in the foyer at the back of the pizzeria. Pastore di Capre was just disappearing through the door at the top of the stairs, his loud protests growing quieter as Pasquale coaxed him inward. Angelina was at her mother's side looking even more disheveled than Giovanna.

"This is where you live?" Giovanna thought.

It was not at all what she'd pictured with each long distance telephone call. Images of American houses from television, of long sweeping staircases that people danced on, rolling green grass with fences and big attached rooms for cars. Those were American homes, not this dank dungeon. She tried to appear satisfied with her decision to accompany her daughter to this strange new world. If this was the life Angelina had been living, then she did not want to add to the stress. But how could the burden of two elderly people, one with a broken mind and one with a broken body, not be adding stress? It was intrinsic in the package.

Giovanna held the railing as though it were a rescue rope. She wasn't sure if the tremors in her arms were a result of fatigue, fear, hunger or the evil eye — *the malocchio* — for the envy was apparent throughout the village when they'd heard she was going to America. She had to be strong — hold back the tears, for Angelina's

157

sake.

"Are you okay?" her daughter asked as they took the last step and stopped on the top landing before walking into the apartment.

Giovanna was breathing heavily. "Yes," she said and paused for a moment. "You know I walk much more than this at home. It's just the difference in time, the travelling. I'm just a bit tired."

"Of course," Angelina said as she guided her mother into the cramped living area. "Remember, Mama—it's temporary."

Giovanna hadn't meant to gasp but she'd thought that there'd be more space and her reflexes weren't what they should have been. The bed pushed against the sofa made for only a few feet around it for walking. The room was a bit darker than she'd expected, given that the sun outside was as bright as the island sun. But only a small stream of yellow light shone through the window above the hotplate.

"Let me sit for a moment. A glass of water, maybe—" Giovanna shuffled to the sofa and sat. "Help your papa. I'm fine." Patrice was at her side in milliseconds holding a bottle of water.

"No, dear. I just want water."

"It's water, Nonna."

"Oh, yes it is."

She took the bottle and struggled with the plastic cap until Patrice reached out and snapped it off. Giovanna didn't like the look of sympathy.

"Where's my little Rocco?" she asked.

"He'll be here soon. Don't worry." Patrice was distracted by her grandfather's ravings in the bedroom. He barely made sense. She hadn't seen him for a while and the difference was jarring.

"Please, Papa." Angelina's voice came from the bedroom also. "Open your mouth. This will help you."

Giovanna met her granddaughter's eyes. They were filled with tears. She patted the sofa beside her. "Come closer, my dear." She thought of Maria and Big Antonio and she sighed as she touched

Patrice's face and then smoothed her hair.

"This is how it is now, but he will calm down when he's rested." Giovanna smiled. "Ah, your nonno—he's a strong one. He's a strong mind, strong body. Don't worry. He's still there. You'll see. When he's rested."

The two hugged and Patrice lingered in the crook of her grandmother's neck. Giovanna patted her head. "My little Patrice. How are you doing here?"

Patrice pulled her head from her grandmother and sat a bit straighter. "I'm good Nonna. Really. I, I met—" she hesitated. Giovanna looked deeper.

"The business?" she asked. "You work many hours your mother tells me. Yes? How is that for you—such a young girl stuck inside four walls all day? Not like Incompresso."

"Oh—the pizza, well really Nonna," Patrice lowered her voice, "I hate the pizza store and I hate pizza," she laughed a quiet laugh. "But I met someone—a boy, well, a man, a young man." She wanted to tell her more but the commotion in the bedroom had escalated.

"He's Italian?" Giovanna asked smiling a slight smile and turning her head toward the bedroom.

"Please Papa!" Angelina's voice was mixed with Pastore di Capre's protests.

"Uh-well," Patrice was formulating a well-organized sales pitch to introduce the idea of Josh when her grandmother pressed down on her thigh and steadied herself there momentarily as she stood up.

"Let me go help your mother," Giovanna said as she made her way to the bedroom.

"Now Pastore, why are you giving Angelina a hard time?"

Pastore di Capre immediately became quiet as he awaited Giovanna's appearance in the doorway. Angelina looked at her mother as she came toward the bed where her father was sitting.

"What is this Carlo nonsense? Who's Carlo?" she asked and

Pastore di Capre instantly began to protest again, his fists in the air as he tried to stand.

"Sit down!" Giovanna yelled at him, "and open your mouth." He complied and Angelina shoved a spoon of applesauce and sedative into his mouth.

"It's something new," Giovanna said to her daughter. "Just don't say the name again. Agree with whatever he says. I'll tell you about it later."

The call about Rocco came through the telephone in the store below. Gina did not have the courage to face Angelina's accusing eyes. Joe was annoyed at her later when he heard how the family had gotten the news. He'd tried to move Rocco through the emergency room as quickly as possible. The intravenous line was usually all that was needed in cases such as his where hydration was the main issue. But the triage nurse had intervened and the doctor on duty admitted Rocco for observation. In the meantime the car was impounded and no one at the pizzeria knew how to deal with that.

Gina thought she was talking to Patrice when Javier's daughter answered the telephone. Patrice was still upstairs in the apartment.

"Patrice, your brother is in the hospital," Gina said.

Javier's daughter could have told her immediately that she was not Patrice but the news of Rocco took her off guard.

Javier's daughter asked, "Why? What's wrong?" And she swallowed back tears.

"He uh, he was admitted this afternoon. He well—I'm sorry Patrice—there's no other way to say it. He had a bad reaction to a drug. It looks like he was, uh—he took—he experimented with some recreational drugs."

"Drugs? Rocco?" Javier's daughter asked.

"Your brother was shooting up, um, I mean he was doing drugs behind a bodega and, uh—well, he was picked up by the police and brought to the hospital. He's going to be okay but—"

Javier's daughter interrupted. "He's not my brother. This isn't Patrice."

"What?" Gina thought of all the patient confidentiality rules she'd just broken and how Joe had told her to go to the store and talk to Angelina personally. She hung up.

"Hello? Hello?"

Javier's daughter was thinking of Rocco in the hospital, helpless and near death under white hospital sheets. He'd need someone to comfort him, someone like her. She pictured herself sitting next to him, holding his hand, mopping his brow. The pizzeria telephone began to ring again and the line of customers standing before her waited not-so-patiently for help. Javier cleared his throat to bring her back to the here-and-now.

"Oh," Javier's daughter went to the pizza oven and grabbed a box from the top of it. She brought it to the customer at the register. "Here you go." The customer wouldn't know it was the wrong pizza until he got home.

The telephone continued to ring. The next customer wanted to pay. Javier mopped the sweat from his brow and continued to throw the pizza dough in the air as he looked over his shoulder and said to his daughter, "go get Patrice."

Javier's daughter texted Patrice, first with her father's request and then: *The hospital called. Rocco overdosed.*

All three—Patrice, Angelina and Pasquale—pushed through the kitchen door moments later and came to the register bumping into each other to get to Javier's daughter first. Her information was vague but Angelina verified it when she called the hospital looking for Rocco.

"Don't say a word about it to Nonna," Angelina said as she put her coat on and headed to the door. "Patrice, you stay down here. And you—" she pointed to Javier's daughter, "Go upstairs and sit with my parents. Come on, Pasquale."

She was thinking about how she needed to learn to drive when suddenly Gina walked through the door.

"Pat," Angelina said in Italian, "Stay here and help Javier. I'll get this one to drive me," She was looking at Gina who actually understood with the few words she knew from her childhood and from Angelina's glare.

Upstairs in the apartment, Javier's daughter tried to explain to Giovanna why it was she who had returned to the apartment rather than Angelina. She held her telephone and punched words into the internet-translator until Nonna thought she understood. Pastore di Capre snored loudly from the other room.

Giovanna quietly asked, "Is my grandson dead?"

Javier's daughter looked perplexed for a moment as she punched her finger on the telephone screen. Then her eyes widened as her forehead creased with lines of worry. "I don't think so," she said mostly to herself and then translated something similar to Giovanna.

Giovanna paced around the room a few times and then stopped at Javier's daughter. They stood facing each other.

"Can that phone make a call to Italy?" she asked in Italian.

Javier's daughter just looked at her.

"Your phone." Giovanna pointed to it.

Javier's daughter handed it to Giovanna. Giovanna looked at the screen for several seconds and handed it back to Javier's daughter. Giovanna thought of Chair's grandson and his attempts at Facetime.

"Why didn't I pay more attention to that?" she thought. Tears began to well. Her frustration and fatigue were wearing her down.

Javier's daughter's eyes widened further. She quickly translated. "Give me a number and I'll call for you."

"Where did I put that?" Giovanna thought. Aloud she said, "My coat. Where's my coat?"

Javier's daughter stood staring, her mouth slightly open—but empty of words as she watched Giovanna walk around the sofa, then the bed, opening and closing the bathroom door, then proceeding to another door that opened to reveal a bedroom. Giovanna sighed loudly and continued to the room in which loud deep snores were emerging. She came out of that room seconds later and handed a folded paper to Javier's daughter. She nodded her head at the girl. Javier's daughter looked at the paper and then at Giovanna.

"Go ahead," Giovanna prompted her as though she were a small child.

Javier's daughter looked at the paper again and back at Giovanna again. Giovanna took the telephone from the girl and wanted to hit her over the head with it but instead she smiled and looked at the screen. Where were the dials, the numbers? It was different than the one Chair's grandson was always trying to get her to use. Instead, Giovanna put the telephone to her ear and said in English, "Hello? Hello? Hello?"

"Oh." Javier's daughter understood. She took the telephone back, looked at the paper in her hand and then began punching the screen. She handed the telephone back to Giovanna.

Giovanna heard Big Antonio's voice.

"Antonio, it's Giovanna. Yes, yes—fine. Just listen. Don't dig the zinnias. You hear me? Do-not-dig-the-zinnias! Do you understand? I cannot explain now. Please, you and Maria are the only ones I trust." She hesitated. "Tell Maria, I'll make it right. Little Antonio—he'll be, um, paid. I promise. I cannot explain right now. Maybe we need—oh, never mind. We'll talk later. The zinnias? You understand? Good. Big kiss and hug for both of you. Yes—yes. We're fine. Don't worry."

Big Antonio's voice was gone. The telephone flashed its digital time: 4:10. Giovanna handed the phone back to Javier's daughter and sat on the sofa and waited. She couldn't help but think of the troupe of people who'd come every day to help her with Pastore di Capre, and the villagers who stopped by just to visit with her, to sit in the garden or help her hang the wash.

The small American apartment suddenly felt warm and the air

too thick to breathe. She closed her eyes and thought of the sea breeze sweeping into the windows and blowing the curtains inward – the fresh, salty brine of the sea – the aroma of jasmine in the evening and the cry of the sea birds overhead.

Giovanna knew that her husband would be waking probably at the precise time everyone else was going to sleep. She felt heavy and tired and lonely.

"What have I done?" she thought, *"What am I doing here?"*

She picked up a pillow and hugged it to her chest. She was sitting with her feet on the floor. She laid her head back onto the sofa cushion and fell into a deep sleep.

It was dark when she awoke to sounds of shuffling within the room. She thought she'd fallen asleep on her sofa on the island. She was holding her infant daughter, Angelina, and the shuffling noise was her young Pastore coming to wake her and bid her to return to their bed. But then the light flicked on and Angelina was an adult, standing beside Pasquale. The young girl with the telephone had disappeared and Patrice was sitting beside her.

"I didn't want to wake you, Mama," Angelina said as Giovanna realized that all three were in sleeping clothes.

"Are you okay?" Patrice asked, "You were crying –" Patrice had more to say but her mother interrupted.

"Let me help you into the room with Papa," she said.

"Papa?" Giovanna was still a bit confused.

"He's sleeping in the other room. Remember? You're in America?" The look that passed between Angelina and Pasquale did not escape Giovanna.

"I know where I am," she said abruptly. "Your papa is still sleeping?"

"I gave him another sedative," Angelina said.

Was this the plan? To keep the two old people as still as possible and tucked away where they could be managed? Giovanna grimaced and her daughter mistook it for pain.

"Do you need something, Mama? For your pain?"

"I have no pain," Giovanna snapped. *"Not physical,"* she thought.

"I only meant for the tremors—I thought it was painful. I didn't mean—"

"No. I'm fine." Giovanna said and knew it was a lie. Her back was fused into a C-shape from sitting so long slumped on a sofa. She tried to stand from the sitting position but wobbled a bit as an electric current shot up her spine into her neck.

"Maybe just a little aspirin," she said as she struggled for breath.

*   *   *   *   *

When Giovanna finally saw her grandson, Rocco, it was several hours later. The morning light was filtering in through the small window above the hotplate. Giovanna had been sleeping in the bedroom in her single bed and was startled by a sudden thud and her husband's cry of shame as the smell of feces permeating every inch of the room. He'd tried to leave his bed in a hurry but had fallen to the floor. The American beds were much taller than theirs at home and Giovanna struggled to get her feet to the floor as Angelina came running into the room. The chairs she'd pushed up to the bedside to prevent such an incident, only served to keep her father wedged between them and the side of the bed as they had slid just the right amount to do so.

Rocco made his entrance just after Pasquale had helped Giovanna bathe Pastore di Capre amid loud protests and curses. Angelina tried to get into the bathroom to help, but Giovanna had pushed her away.

"There are certain things a daughter should not have to do for her father," she'd said and wondered, *"Where is Rocco?"*

The apartment door was open as were the bedroom windows and the small window above the hotplate. Giovanna coaxed Pastore di Capre to the sofa. Wearing a pair of Rocco's sweat pants that were rolled up to his ankles and pulled tightly around his waist and an oversized sweatshirt, Pastore di Capre looked like a small child. As Giovanna led him to the sofa, she put a large black comb in his hand, and she looked up at Patrice who stood nearby with eyes that were a mixture of horror and sorrow.

"Close the windows," Giovanna said. "He'll catch his death all wet like this." And for the first time she contemplated that idea.

Patrice crinkled her nose, "but the smell—"

Angelina interrupted. "Go close the bedroom windows," she said as she began to turn the little crank that pulled the small window above the hotplate closed.

At that moment, footsteps were heard downstairs in the foyer.

Pastore di Capre was trying to convey something to Giovanna as she sat him on the sofa and helped him run the comb through his hair.

"Up on the, after we—come to and then around here." He circled his free hand in front of her, large circles in a desperate plea.

"Yes, yes okay." Giovanna responded.

"What does he want?" Patrice's throat felt as though it had a rubber ball lodged near her windpipe.

Giovanna looked at her granddaughter with sorrowful eyes and shrugged her shoulders. "I have no idea," she said softly.

The footsteps started up the stairs and there were obviously more than one person's.

Pastore di Capre began waving his hands up and down, his voice became louder as he tried to make himself understood and then suddenly he stopped and stared and then smiled and said, "Ah! There's my Rocco!" as he quickly stood up from the sofa. And everyone turned to the doorway where Rocco was entering with Gina behind him.

Giovanna looked at Patrice and they both smiled as Angelina ran to her father laughing.

"Ha! You old goat." She kissed his head lightly, and said, "You know your grandson, eh?"

Her eyes welled with tears. It was a happy few seconds before Pastore di Capre hit her hard with the back of his hand and began his rant of indecipherable phrases again.

"Oh God." Gina gasped and ran to Angelina as Angelina backed away.

"You can help him." Angelina said to her as she pulled her hand from the sting of her cheek.

Rocco was pale but smiled and went to his grandfather.

"Whoa, Nonno what are you doing?" He rubbed the old man's shoulder as if he were a pet and helped him to sit back onto the sofa. Giovanna was sitting on the sofa with the comb in her hand, watching Rocco.

Rocco met his father's eyes. Pasquale was buttoning up a shirt. He ignored his son and said to Patrice, "Let's go downstairs. Javier needs our help."

"Papa."

Rocco wanted to say more but his father brushed past him and was out the door. Patrice looked at Rocco and touched his arm as she passed him and followed her father. But she said nothing.

Gina was absorbing Angelina's comment, "Me? How can I help?"

Pastore di Capre was speaking to Rocco. "Ah Rocco, you're here. We have after the—and around, and then we go." His eyes shone with the light from the small window above the hotplate. "So after dinner? Is dark and there we have. Okay?"

"Huh?" Rocco looked to his mother for help but she was answering Gina.

Angelina said, "You're a speech pathologist, yes? Patrice looked it up on the phone—after your husband left the pizzeria. You remember what he said?"

"Well, yes but—"

"You heard my father, just now. How clearly he said *there's my Rocco*?"

"Yes, but," Gina hesitated. She really had not heard any such thing for it was all done in Italian. "It's probably a phrase he said all his life. It doesn't work that way. I cant—"

Pastore di Capre raised his voice waiting for Rocco's response. "Eh? Okay? We have the—to go the, around and then okay?"

Rocco shifted his weight and looked at his mother and then back at his grandfather. "Ah Nonno—what do you mean? What are you saying?"

"Just agree with him. Say 'yes, okay.' Nod your head." Giovanna said to her grandson as she stood and lightly kissed Rocco on both cheeks. "What's happened to you? You look sick?" She was thinking of the life they must have been living here and she shook her head lightly. *"Why? Why would they trade Incompresso for this?"*

"No, I'm okay," Rocco answered her.

"You're not okay. You need some meat, some vegetables, some sleep. Is there a kitchen I can cook in?"

Angelina heard her mother and looked away from Gina for a moment to answer her.

"I told you, Mama. It's temporary. I'll cook something downstairs. I'll bring it up here." To Gina she said, "But your husband said—the day in the pizzeria—he said you could help my parents."

"You misunderstood." Gina said. "Your mother, maybe she has Parkinson's. There's a treatment for that—for the tremors, to reduce them. He mentioned me because I work with brain-injured people. I help them communicate. But your father, he needs someone who speaks his language and well, you know, it sounds like dementia and that's not, um, well—I can't—"

But she didn't finish as Pastore di Capre somehow felt the tension in his wife who stood in front of him speaking quietly to Rocco. Not so much as felt it but perceived something like fear as an animal might and so he reacted thus.

As he tried to stand he said, "You there, boy!" He was looking at Gina, "get the shovel, go up—when no one, and—" His face was red and he had pulled himself off the sofa. Despite Rocco's attempt to soothe him, he began to flail his arms. "And I tell you, with a shovel—go and around." He was yelling.

"Do you have something to calm him?" Gina said above the commotion.

"Rocco," Angelina said in Italian, "Grab some applesauce from the refrigerator." She looked at her mother, "Mama, try to talk to him."

"No!" Giovanna knew what the applesauce was for. "No more of that. It makes him worse."

"We'll take him to a doctor, Mama. It's temporary."

"No. No, please!"

For the first time in his life, Rocco saw his grandmother cry as he handed his mother a small plastic cup of applesauce and she ran to the bedroom to retrieve a pill. He watched as his grandmother put herself between his grandfather and his mother. His grandmother pleaded like a child as his mother pushed her aside and yelled at his grandfather. Pastore di Capre recognized the danger and suddenly put a protective hand across Giovanna's chest to save her from the attacker, as clearly Angelina's manner had indicated it was she who meant them harm. He had no idea the attacker was his daughter. It was instinct that put his arm in a protective position. And that momentary focus on his wife allowed the *attacker* to overpower him.

Pastore di Capre gagged as the spoon hit his throat and then he spit the applesauce, a direct hit in Angelina's eyes which then welled with tears and she began to sob as she screamed, "open your mouth, old man!" in Italian. She held the medication bottle in one hand and the spoon in the other, a mix of applesauce and saliva dripped from her nose.

"Everyone calm down!" Gina yelled above the commotion, which produced quiet from everyone except Pastore di Capre. "Just let him stand up and rave. He's feeding on your panic. Let him walk around and say what he wants. You need to stay calm and he will feel the environment."

They were all looking at her. "And even if he doesn't calm down, so what?" she continued. "Just make sure he doesn't hurt himself."

"What's she saying?" Giovanna whispered but Rocco and Angelina were listening to Gina. Pastore di Capre was yelling syllables and words as he walked toward her.

"There are things you can do for him," she smiled at him and kept her voice even, "but this is not the time to talk about it. Stay calm. Be careful with that medication, Angelina—use it only as your doctor instructed or it can do damage, even be fatal."

"What's *fatal*?" Rocco asked his mother in Italian?

"She means too much of the medication can kill him." Angelina answered and Giovanna looked at her and then at the medication bottle.

A few minutes later, Angelina walked Gina down the stairs and stopped in the foyer. "How can I repay you? For Rocco—you know—the hospital, and the car?"

"Don't worry about it."

"When things calm down, we'll cook a nice meal for you and your husband."

"Maybe," Gina was thinking of the support group her mother had been pestering her about. "We'll see. For now, just look into that place I told you about. It's expensive—but you need someone to look after your father while you figure out what you're going to do."

"Yes." Angelina thought of the house. Her shoulders stooped from the weight of it. And what about Rocco?

"How can we help Rocco?" she asked Gina.

"You need to talk to *him* about it. He's the only one who can deal with that."

Gina had spoken to him a bit in the car on her way from the hospital to the pizzeria. Heroine was no joke. He was lucky to be alive but it wouldn't last long if he didn't get a grip. He was more a child than the man she'd thought him. And well—after Joe pointed out the obvious, her desire to be at the pizzeria fizzled and left her flat. Now as she looked at Angelina and thought to tell her about an Alzheimer's support group at the hospital, she realized the hypocrisy of it and decided she'd give her mother a call about that bereavement group when she got home.

"One more thing," Gina hesitated, "about that medication."

"Yes?" Angelina waited but Gina took a moment to continue.

"Well, it's actually something that many addicts use. Sometimes they crush it up and sniff it. I'm just saying—"

Gina was interrupted by the back door to the pizzeria as it opened and Javier's daughter stuck her head in.

"I was in the kitchen," she said as she nodded her head in the direction of the open door. "I heard voices—uh, I was just wondering, well, um how's Rocco?"

"I'm fine." Rocco answered her and all three heads swept up to the landing at the top of the stairs. He'd been quietly listening to his mother and Gina. He'd heard about the expensive place for his grandfather. And about the medication. He was looking at Javier's daughter with a slight smile.

"I'm just fine, girl."

CHAPTER 12

It didn't take Giovanna long to realize what was happening with her grandson, Rocco. She wanted to find a way to talk to him about it but they never seemed to be alone. Now, they stood at the entrance of *the place* Gina had suggested for Pastore di Capre.

Rocco had driven her in the car that Joe had helped them get out of impound. On the drive over, Rocco had been quiet and Giovanna had been wrapped up in thoughts of her ailing husband. She decided she'd speak to Rocco on the way back home. It was Giovanna's first time to *the place* — though Pastore di Capre had been there three days already. Yes, it was a lovely place with lots of flowers in the courtyard and a beautiful wooden door at the entrance that was inlaid with carvings. It reminded Giovanna of a church.

Rocco held the door open for her as she made her way with the cane that Angelina insisted she use. As she clip-clopped over the tile floor she worried about how the cane might make her look like a feeble old woman. She stopped and brought her free hand to the gray hairs of her head and smoothed them neatly. Then she raised her chin and proceeded through the door.

The place had a high sweeping ceiling with an ornate chandelier hanging from the middle of a dome. The reception desk was the original mahogany wood that had been kept exactly as it was when *the place* had been a hotel back in the 1920s. It sat before a long sweeping window that led to a garden. The mahogany's shellacked-shine from several attempts at refurbishing held the reflection of the window and gave the receptionist a glow—or if one happened to suffer from cataracts as did most of the residents, it was more of a glare.

Rocco had helped his mother get Pastore di Capre situated so he knew that his grandfather was on the top floor. It hadn't been easy to leave his grandfather there, especially knowing that no one understood Italian but the Italian Nonno Pastore spoke was mostly incomprehensible so it didn't seem to matter. It didn't occur to Rocco that Pastore di Capre would now, not only be unable to communicate clearly but would not be able to comprehend anything that was being said around him.

The elevator doors opened and the two walked into a large room that was meant to look like an open kitchen, dining room and living area of a home—an American home. The nurse, who sat behind a desk that was built into a kitchen counter, greeted them.

"Good morning," she said, "Buenos dias!" She smiled a big smile at Giovanna showing off her knowledge of another language—knowing Giovanna was the wife of that foreign man in room 4.

Giovanna looked up at her grandson for clarification. She knew the words *good morning* but that other word?

"She means *buon giorno*." Rocco said to his grandmother.

"Good morning," Rocco directed his greeting to the woman and took the pen from her so he could sign their names into the book that lay flat on the countertop.

There were several doors that led to bedrooms off of that living area. The wallpaper and paintings, the sofas and overstuffed armchairs, the side tables, coffee tables and magazine racks were all an attempt to have it look like a living room in a home so as not to confuse the residents. It was the American home design

Giovanna had expected her daughter's family to be living within. But it looked nothing like their home on Incompresso.

She watched several silver-haired people as they moved slowly about the area, some with walkers, some with canes—like her. They reminded her of the dull silver snails that inched their way over the harbor rocks without any apparent direction.

Giovanna followed Rocco to room number four.

A woman in a white uniform, not much younger than Giovanna, was sitting with Pastore di Capre at the window next to the bed. She turned when they came in and spoke in perfect Italian.

"Hi, you must be Mr. Pietro's wife. I'm Gia." She said.

"Mr. Pietro?" Giovanna asked, though she was thrilled to know there was an Italian nurse there for her husband.

Pastore di Capre turned toward his wife with heavy eyelids that opened a bit wider when he saw her. He looked from Giovanna to Rocco.

"Ah, there's my Rocco," he said slowly with a bit of a slur as he tried to stand.

Rocco went to him and helped him navigate around the chair as Giovanna said to the other woman, "We call him Pastore. Does he answer to Pietro?"

The other woman, Gia, did not answer the question but she said, "well, it's nice to meet you," and she stuck her hand out to Giovanna.

"Gia is short for Giovanna?" It was a question without a need for an answer, "I'm Gia also—Giovanna." Giovanna smiled as she shook the woman's hand and looked at her husband.

"So, how is he doing?"

"Okay, I guess. You have to talk to the doctor, or one of the nurses."

"You're not a nurse?"

Rocco had Pastore di Capre by the arm and was walking away from the women. He was glad to see his grandfather calmer. He reached up and wiped a bit of saliva from Pastore di Capre's chin, using his own sleeve. Pastore di Capre looked down at his feet as he slowly put one foot in front of the other and leaned into Rocco. He made a few grunts and groans, but no words.

"No, I'm not a nurse," Gia answered Giovanna. "I work in the kitchen. My shift is about to start. One of the nurses came down the day before yesterday to see if I could help communicate with Mr. Piet—uh, Mr. Pastore."

"Good Lord," Giovanna said quietly and thought, "*It must have been awful for him.*"

A cool shadow passed over Gia's face. She misunderstood and thought, "*Well, kitchen work is good honest work—and likely as important as nursing in a place like this.*"

She watched as Giovanna turn her back to look at Pastore di Capre.

A dagger dipped in guilt was lodged in Giovanna's breastbone. She saw her grandson and her husband reach the bedroom door. Their pace was slow—two more snails on the harbor rocks. As they disappeared out into the living area, she turned back to Gia and said with a small smile, "Well, he's calm now."

"Yes," Gia's rigid jaw barely allowed the word to escape through her clenched teeth.

"I came up yesterday to see him also. It's lucky I'm here to help—someone to speak to him in Italian when you leave him here alone." The last few words dug deeply into Giovanna's flesh, as they were meant to do.

Gia continued, "I'm from a Piacenza, just outside of Milano. You know it?"

Giovanna thought a moment. "Yes, of course I know Milano, but Pia—"

Gia interrupted her. "Your accent. What is it? From where?"

"Incompresso. A small island in the Adriatic—it's a bit—"

"I know it," again Gia interrupted. "*Il sud*—the south." She spoke the words as if she were drinking vinegar. "I have to get to

175

work."

Gia stood abruptly. Giovanna looked at this other woman in confusion—a *sister* from her homeland—hurling an insult that landed like a slap. Its subtle force shocked Giovanna. The woman had started out so friendly. Why the change?

As a formality and with the ingrained habit of island hospitality, Giovanna said, "It was nice to meet you."

Gia did not respond. She pulled a small smile onto her face and smoothed the front of her kitchen uniform with her hands. Then she walked from the room with Giovanna following. Giovanna watched her walk to the elevator and then she went to find her grandson and her husband.

Rocco had helped Pastore di Capre to the outdoor sitting area, which was a green rooftop garden. Giovanna could see them from the windows of the giant French doors. Pastore di Capre's eyes were closed, his mouth open wide and his head lying back on the cushion of an overstuffed outdoor sofa. Rocco sat next to him looking at nothing.

When he saw his grandmother emerge, he smiled.

"Looks like you found a friend," he said. "Good to have someone from home to talk to, heh?"

"She's not from home," Giovanna snapped and she sat in a chair opposite the two men.

She looked more closely at the rooftop garden where several other people sat. A large tree thick with leaves, so thick that not even the smallest ray of sun could find its way through, hung over the garden like a cloud. Sitting under it, Giovanna felt a sense of isolation. The sunny day was obvious in the world outside its perimeter, alive with young contrasting colors, but not so, beneath the canopy of leaves.

A shimmering thread of silk just beyond the leafy perimeter ran from the window beside the French doors and into the tarp of leaves. Giovanna's eyes followed it and she was grateful for whatever genetic combination it was that had given her such crisp vision at her age, allowing her to see the intricate web along the silver line. She watched a spider skillfully waiting without movement, waiting for the unsuspecting travelers flying on the breeze, small and insignificant as they became tangled in the web.

She saw them both—the strong and the weak, their well-defined roles in nature's plan—and she watched as the web vibrated with the twisting frenzy of the captives. But try as they might, their wings became silent as they accepted their fate and succumbed to the finality of the web.

"What are you looking at?" Rocco asked.

"Nothing, really," she answered. But she had reached a decision, one that she had been grappling with since Pastore di Capre had been taken from her side in the small apartment. She leaned in close to Rocco and spoke.

"My sweet boy," she said, "I want to tell you about something that is part of our ancestry."

"I've heard about it, Nonna. It's the *black luck*, right? Don't bother—it's nonsense."

"I couldn't agree more," she said with a sad smile. "Now listen."

Rocco moved forward and rested his elbows on his knees. He waited.

"Yes, there are those who say you were cursed with the black luck," Giovanna began.

"Because I was born during an earthquake." Rocco nodded his head. He'd heard it plenty of times and one had to wonder whether or not his actions that day outside the mainland bar had just been a culmination of the beliefs he'd been fed and his unconscious will to fulfill them.

Giovanna reached over and put her hand on her grandson's arm.

"There is no black luck. I think you and I agree on that, right?" Rocco nodded his head lightly and Giovanna continued. "Nor are there protective angels hovering over us."

She thought of her hours in church, the novenas and the lit candles. She looked at her husband, still sound asleep with a small line of saliva escaping the corner of his mouth as his head lay limp on the sofa cushion.

"Rocco, there *is* hard work and planning and opportunity. And I am going to lay opportunity at your feet right now. Whether you choose to trample it underfoot or pick it up and cradle it—well, that is your choice. There is nothing more I can do for you. Now listen carefully. A few months ago—no, it was before your mother went to America, oh my it was over a year ago—Big Antonio came to me with a pouch filled with gold coins."

Rocco's eyebrows lifted and he was about to say something but Giovanna held her hand up.

"Listen, Rocco—be silent and listen. You know, Little Antonio, he was fishing for octopus near the rocks on the far side of the island. It's been difficult for the fishermen these last few years. The sea is not what it used to be, the plastic and the pollution, well—so he's been relying on the octopus for some time but they're hard to find on the harbor side—everyone looks for octopus over there. So he took his boat to the rocky side. He's a careful man and he knows what he's doing. One day he found a pouch with some gold coins. They were wedged between two of the boulders and well—you can imagine his excitement but he was also very cautious."

Rocco nodded and waited for his grandmother to continue. Pastore di Capra snorted a few times and opened his eyes. He lifted his head and looked around at the garden. Giovanna stood slowly. She was looking at her husband but talking quietly to her grandson.

"Those gold coins were your grandfather's," she said, "and so—they are rightfully yours." She was standing now, "There's more to it, but you must not share this story with anyone. Do you understand?"

Pastore di Capre was leaning forward, his hands gripping the sofa as he tried to stand but Rocco's hand was on his knee, "Wait, Nonno," he said to his grandfather though he was looking at his grandmother—his heart racing. He reached out and grabbed her wrist as she clopped her way toward Pastore di Capre with her cane clinking against the cement.

"Wait." Rocco looked at his grandmother, "Wha-what-what are you saying? How do you know they're Nonno's coins? Where are they now? Nonna? Did—did you—did you bring them?" The thoughts in his head were colliding with the words in his mouth.

"Not now. I'll explain." She lowered her voice, "not in front of Nonno Pastore."

Rocco lost his grip on his grandfather's knee as Pastore di Capre stood. Giovanna was standing in front of her husband. She smiled.

"Gia," he said and returned her smile.

Giovanna wondered if he knew her or if it was the other woman he wanted. She took his hand as Rocco slowly stood next to them. Quietly, she said to Rocco, "Take us back to the apartment above the store. Just for a visit. He's calm and I want to sit with him—just for a few moments, to feel like a family again." She looked at Rocco. They were standing very close. "Will you do that for me?"

He nodded.

"Yes, of course," the nurse at the desk said, as she punched a combination into the buttons next to the elevator. "He's not required to stay. You can take him on a walk or a visit to town or anywhere you want." She smiled as the three disappeared behind the closing elevator doors.

Giovanna could feel the tension in Rocco's arm as she held it momentarily to readjust the cane in her other hand. Rocco looked at her and said nothing but his eyes were filled with questions.

She whispered, "Little Antonio showed the pouch to his father. It was obvious the coins were old and when Big Antonio found a chain with a Saint Antonio medal at the bottom of the pouch, he knew they were your grandfather's because he recognized where he'd carved an inscription on the back—two horns to ward off *malocchio*. It was a medal he'd given to Nonno Pastore's mother to give him when he returned from the war. Big Antonio has an exact matching medal."

The elevator doors opened.

"Where are they now? The coins." Rocco asked but Giovanna was already out of the elevator. Rocco helped his grandfather forward as he held the elevator doors open for a few people entering it. Giovanna clip-clopped her way to the facility entrance. She turned and waited for Rocco and Pastore di Capre.

"The pouch is buried in the yard—in my yard—on Incompresso," she said quietly as Rocco held the facility door open for her.

As she passed by him into a large foyer between the outdoors and the reception desk she said, "They're yours, Rocco. Go get them. Only Big Antonio, Maria and their son know about them."

Rocco helped his grandparents into the back seat of the car as he pictured his grandmother's front yard dug up and the pouch gone. He couldn't believe that anyone would leave a pouch of gold buried in the ground, especially now that Nonna was so far from home and so old and frail. As they drove toward the highway, Rocco let his imagination run wild.

"Ah! What I could do with such treasure!" he thought.

He looked in the rearview mirror at his grandparents in the back seat. Nonno Pastore was asleep again, his head leaning on Nonna Giovanna's shoulder. His grandmother's eyes were closed also, but Rocco wasn't sure if she was asleep.

"This has to be a tale she's telling me." He thought, *"It can't be real. She's probably losing her mind also—with the traveling and at her age. No—these gold coins aren't real."*

Giovanna's eyes opened slowly and she met Rocco's in the rearview mirror. As if she had guessed his thoughts she said, "Rocco, when your grandfather was a young man, when he came back from the war, he had a friend with him—someone he'd met in the war. No one knew much about this man but Nonno was fiercely loyal to him," she hesitated, "until one day, the man was—well it looks like your grandfather might have—" She changed her mind. She wouldn't say it. There was no reason to muddy her husband's image in his grandson's eyes. "I believe Nonno Pastore got the gold coins from him. And—"

Rocco was looking in the rearview mirror and back at the road, back and forth, road—mirror—road—mirror, until he pulled the car to the side of the road, pushed the gear into park and turned around to face his grandmother.

"Go on," he said.

"Well," Giovanna continued. "Big Antonio knew that was his medal. And those types of coins haven't been used for many years. And the pouch, made of goatskin, was—it was something the *friend* had a talent for—making things from the skin of the goats. He'd made a larger goatskin bag for a woman he was supposed to marry. And he'd put his initials on the bottom. This pouch, Rocco, it had the man's initials on the bottom."

"Then it belongs to that man," Rocco said.

"Perhaps." Giovanna answered and she glanced sideways at Pastore di Capre who stirred momentarily, his head still resting on her shoulder. Giovanna reached up and caressed her husband's head. She looked at Rocco, "but I believe the pouch was a gift and the coins are somehow related to that friend's death."

"He's dead?"

"It was an accident. He supposedly fell into a ravine."

"Supposedly?"

"That part is not important, Rocco. The man is dead and as far as we know, he had no family."

Rocco looked at his frail old grandfather and narrowed his eyes. "Hm. Maybe you're right," he said as he looked back at Giovanna, "But why would Big Antonio's son hand them over. He found them. And why would he leave them buried in your yard for no one to use. You and Nonno are gone—why shouldn't they dig them up? Maybe they've already done it."

"No, Big Antonio and Maria—they're from the old ways—they would never deceive me. They're not thieves. And Little Antonio—well, his father verified that he gave Nonno that Saint Antonio medal—Little Antonio has no reason to not believe his father. He's always been a good boy. He's not a thief either."

"So, why bury the pouch then? Why not just put it in a drawer."

"Well—Big Antonio and his family are not thieves but that doesn't mean there are none on the island. We've had people in and out of the house these last few weeks—some I barely knew— coming to help me with Nonno." She heaved a heavy sigh. "It was much better there for both of us, but—well, there was no way for me to know what it was like over here. And—" Another heavy sigh, "well, I just kept hoping we could find an answer for our *problems* and I missed having your mother." Giovanna's eyes became wet, "And you, and Patrice." She put her hand to her eyes and closed them for a moment. Rocco remained silent—waiting.

"And Rocco—Nonno Pastore saw the pouch lying on the kitchen table once and flew into such a rage. We thought it would bring him some relief, knowing it had been found, but his reaction—well that's when we decided to bury it in the yard. It's where I used to plant the zinnias. And I promised Little Antonio half."

Rocco's eyebrows lifted. Giovanna continued. "If he hadn't found them, there'd be none," she said. "They were supposed to dig them up after we left. I wasn't sure what we were going to do with the other half. I thought we'd be going back—" Her voice trailed off.

Rocco was confused. "But you *are* going back, Nonna, aren't you? After some kind of treatment?"

"I don't think that's what your mother wants."

"Well, what do you want?"

"*I want my youth back, my husband to be whole, my world to make sense,*" she thought, but aloud she said, "Well, I *do* want to go back but I'm not sure what's right anymore. Maybe we'll see what happens with the medicine that Nonno gets for his broken brain."

"Well, you *can* go back, Nonna." Rocco turned to face forward and put the car back in drive. "If that's what you want, I'll bring you. Just tell me—anytime. Any day."

Nonna Giovanna looked at him in the rearview mirror and smiled but said nothing as the car pulled back onto the road. She stared out the window, her mind searching, calculating.

"Rocco, dear?"

"Yes?"

"Do they have those little mints over here, the little white ones Nonno likes?"

"Uh," Rocco was trying to remember what it was his grandfather liked.

"You know? The ones in the little square box. Tiny little white mints?"

"Oh, yeah. Sure. Why? Do you want some?"

"Would you mind?" Giovanna asked in a small voice. "I think he would like that." She smoothed Pastore di Capre's hair with her hand and kissed him lightly on the forehead.

CHAPTER 13

Angelina had gotten the call from Rocco and now she was straightening up the apartment when she suddenly realized her father's medication was gone. She pulled drawer after drawer out, knelt on the floor and looked under all the beds, swept the broom handle beneath the sofa and along the cabinet near the little window — but no medication bottle rolled out.

The doctor at the facility had not been able to completely read the label, which was partially written in Italian, though he knew the medication. "It's a bit too strong," he'd said. "And well — I'm not going to allow a medication that I did not prescribe. We'll give him something a bit more appropriate."

Angelina had accepted the doctor's decision and simply brought the medication bottle back to the apartment. She thought she'd left it on the night table next to her mother's twin bed. She looked one more time, crouching down low to see under the bed and then under the night table, before she heard the commotion on the stairs and ran to the door to help her son. She narrowed her eyes and looked at Rocco with an intensity that caused him to look quickly behind at the cluttered foyer and then back at his mother.

"What?" he asked.

Angelina shook her head and said nothing. She descended the

stairs to help her mother as Rocco led Pastore di Capre step by step upward.

"I set up a small table in the living room." She said as she took her mother's hand and walked upward. "Pat is making something for us. Rocco told me you wanted some time as a family and—"

"That sounds lovely." Giovanna was out of breath. She stopped on a step, which caused Rocco and Pastore di Capre, behind her, to stop also.

"Could we please just talk for a moment when we get up there," Giovanna said, "we can eat later but maybe Papa and I could rest together in the bedroom a bit first. I'd like it if you could push those two beds together. Make it one—like at home. I just want to lie next to him for a while. We'll just—"

She had to stop for the tears began to well in her eyes and her throat felt as if it were made of cotton. She couldn't push one more word from it.

"Oh Mama. It's okay—okay. Come on. Let's continue up. Whatever you want. We'll do whatever you want."

Angelina was overcome with her own guilt. She remembered her parents in younger years. They were kind and loving to each other. She thought of herself and Pasquale and the ironworks bench. Of course, her mother yearned for the closeness of the man she loved. How could she have been so blind?

When they got to the top of the landing, Giovanna stopped a moment as Rocco and Pastore di Capre passed by. Angelina could feel the trembling of her mother's arm as she held her. "I have an appointment for you, Mama—for some therapy for your tremors."

Giovanna looked at Angelina. "Therapy?"

"It's called *deep brain stimulation*."

"What?!" Giovanna looked at Angelina in horror. She grabbed Angelina's other hand. "This sounds like gypsy medicine."

"No, no—really, Mama. It's something. I read about it and they do it at the hospital where Rocco—eh," she cleared her throat but was unable to finish.

"Let's go in." Giovanna nodded toward the apartment entrance where Rocco and Pastore di Capre were just making their way around the sofa. "Make some coffee—strong. We'll talk about it."

Pastore di Capre sat at the table. When Angelina put a cup of coffee in front of him, he looked up at her.

"Biscuit?" he asked. Back on Incompresso, there was always one of Giovanna's baked goods to go with his coffee.

Angelina patted her father's head and said to Rocco, who was just about to sit down with his coffee, "grab my purse over there. I have a biscotti in there."

Giovanna saw the loving pat on the head. It should have comforted her or given her a sense of well being but instead it saddened her to see her husband reduced to a child under the hand of their own child. She lifted her cup to drink but the angle of her elbow to the table didn't allow her to anchor it on the flat surface, as she'd become accustomed to doing at home. So the tremors were more pronounced as she brought the rim to her mouth. For Giovanna, the look on her daughter's face was more disturbing than the pat on Pastore di Capre's head.

"Angelina, what is it you want here—in America? In this pizzeria?"

"Well, Mama. It's a bit complicated. It *had been* a good plan. You yourself agreed with it."

"That's true," Giovanna said, "but I didn't know. Now I see it and—"

"It's not that simple. Our money is tied up in this place and now in a new house."

Pastore di Capre slurped at his coffee and broke the biscotti into pieces on the table.

"Why the house?" Giovanna asked.

"Well—it's an investment." Angelina cleared her throat. "I'm not sure I want to go back quite yet." She was thinking of the treatment for her mother. "I—I—I'm just not sure what I want."

"And yet you buy a house? Something so permanent?"

Rocco brushed some of the biscotti crumbs away from his cup. Pastore di Capre crushed a small piece into dust and rubbed his finger in a circular movement on the table.

Rocco looked at his mother and said, "Well, I have some news—sort of. I was, um, thinking of going back."

Angelina's head snapped up and she looked at him with searing daggers, "You?!" She let out a quick short stream of air, "Is this a joke? Why do you think we're here in the first place?" her voice got louder. "Who do you think this is all for?" She hit her hand down on the table.

Pastore di Capre looked up suddenly.

Giovanna grabbed Angelina's arm, "Now, calm down." She looked at her grandson and then at Angelina. "What if you hadn't done this," she asked. "What would you have done? How do you suppose your life would have been?"

Both Angelina and Rocco were silent. Rocco stared at the crumbs in front of him. *How would it have been if you hadn't done this?* He'd asked himself that a million times since he'd been locked away. What if he and his friends had never boarded the ferry undetected. What if he hadn't gotten involved with the incident outside the bar on the mainland? His life changed in a matter of seconds after he'd emerged from Incompresso's cocoon—from a boy to a murderer—a horrific metamorphosis.

It was Rocco's instinct but also his inexperience that had driven the knife into the older man. And it was chance—not black luck—that led the knife to an artery. When Rocco had gone outside to urinate in the bushes behind the dark club, he'd heard the woman's muffled pleas as her face was pressed up against the building. At first Rocco wasn't sure what he was looking at until the thrusting of the white buttocks sent him a vision of the goats on the ridge. One goat mounting the other, thrusting in and out while the female let out intermittent bleating. Suddenly he understood and reacted with a punch to the man's head. It all happened so fast. The knife blade coming toward him, the woman's screams, the glint of metal against cement as Rocco scrambled to retrieve the knife and then as the fist came toward his face, he thrust forward and felt the blade sink into dough-like flesh. The woman testified against him in court. Next to the judge, she sat with her hands in her lap, as her starched black suit shook with her sobs and she described how the young thug—pointing to Rocco—had attacked them and killed her boyfriend.

Rocco pushed a few small crumbs toward his grandfather and closed his eyes tightly. He shook his head hard once and opened his eyes to see his mother looking at him. Her eyes had softened. She'd been thinking of England and of the trip they never got to take together.

"Well?" Giovanna was waiting for an answer. "What would you like to do?"

"It's not that simple, Mama."

"I know," Giovanna said as she shook her head slowly. "And now look what's happened—you have two old parents burdening you."

"No, no—that's not it. It's just that—that, well. We're not as free as you think we are."

"My dear little girl, freedom is not something that is given or taken. It's inside you and it's your choice how much of it you will allow yourself."

"*That's ridiculous,*" Angelina thought, "*You have no idea what life is like now. It's not like your time at all – in your little island nest.*"

To her mother she said, "Maybe you're right. Let's talk about you and Papa. About your treatment."

"Not now," Giovanna said, "Help Papa to the bedroom. We want to lie down for a little while. We can eat afterwards and then we can discuss whatever you want."

Angelina looked at Rocco, "Did you by any chance, see Nonno's medication we brought with us from Incompresso?"

"Not that again," Giovanna said. "No more of that. Please! Can't you see he's better without it?"

"I'm just asking because I—"

"Please," Giovanna interrupted her. "Rocco, help me with your nonno."

Angelina decided to wait until after her father had returned to the facility to talk to Rocco.

Rocco pushed the two beds together as his grandmother had asked and helped his grandfather onto one. Giovanna pulled herself up onto the other bed and made her way to the middle.

"Help me with these pillows, will you?"

Rocco and Angelina helped her place the pillows in the exact position that would allow her and Pastore di Capre to sit up against the headboard and next to each other in the middle of the two beds.

When Rocco was close to her, Giovanna said quietly, "don't forget my zinnias."

"What zinnias?" Angelina asked. "Did you leave flowers in the car?" She looked at Rocco.

"It's nothing," Giovanna said quickly, "just a little private matter between a nonna and her grandson." She winked at Rocco and moved closer to Pastore di Capre.

Angelina watched her mother take her father's hand and kiss it gently. Then Giovanna laid her head against Pastore di Capre's shoulder and he smiled a smile his daughter hadn't seen in months. She shook her head and motioned to Rocco to follow her.

"I get it," she thought, *"they just want to be husband and wife as best they can. So be it. Let them have their moment before he has to go back to the facility."*

She said, "Mama, when do you want me to wake you?"

"Would you mind terribly if we didn't eat? Could Papa stay here just for the night?"

Angelina had to admit, he was much calmer than in previous days. Maybe that doctor was right about the medication from Italy. The medication. Rocco. She wanted to give her mother as much calm time as possible. As much as she wanted to talk to

Rocco about it now, she knew it would be better to wait.

"Sure," said Angelina as she and Rocco left the room and she quietly closed the door.

Giovanna's head rested on Pastore di Capre's shoulder and she could hear the gentle rhythm of his heartbeat. It was strong. She started to hum with the beat and then the hum became a song— one she'd sung a million times in church. Pastore di Capre picked up the words of the song as instinct kicked in and their small thin voices clung together in the bedroom air.

Angelina heard them through the door as she stood with Rocco.

"Let's go downstairs and help with the dinner rush," she said.

Pastore di Capre's voice became breathy as they continued to sing. He followed Giovanna's rhythm and looked down at their hands entwined. He took his other hand and caressed the back of Giovanna's trembling fingers before he enclosed them within his both hands. With her free hand, Giovanna reached into the top of her dress and she stopped singing, but Pastore di Capre continued. Her hand searched along the lining of her brassiere until she found what she was looking for and she pulled out the medication.

Pastore di Capre did not see Giovanna's face streaked with tears as she reached into the pocket of her dress and found the mints Rocco had bought. The rattling of the plastic container caused Pastore di Capre to stop singing. He waited a moment while Giovanna pulled her hand from his and fumbled with the paper seal. Then she shook two mints free and brought them to Pastore di Capre's lips. He took them and as he chewed, Giovanna opened the medication and spilled a few pills into her palm. She put two pills to his lips and he took those in, chewing, mixing them with the mints. He crinkled his nose, stopped chewing for a moment and then resumed. Giovanna continued giving him pills mixed with mints until Pastore di Capre's breathing became raspy and his heart slowed. Then she emptied the rest of the pills into her own mouth and mashed them into a bitter bolus. As they made their way down her throat, she had thoughts of regret, until she heard Pastore di Capre speak to her in clear strong words.

"What are we doing here?" he said as he lifted her head and looked into her eyes. "It's a beautiful day. We shouldn't be wasting it in this dark room."

He jumped from the bed with the spring of a twenty-year-old and pushed the shutters open as Giovanna made her way to the edge of the bed. The sun poured into the small bedroom and the breeze blew Giovanna's honey brown hair into her eyes. Pastore di Capre came and stood in front of her. He held her two hands and helped her to her feet where the warm stone floor held their bare soles. Then he kissed her on the mouth, their lips as soft as rose pedals melding together.

The bedroom door opened and the sunlight blinded them as they walked through the living room out into the garden. The sea birds' songs, long and loud, sang a welcoming hymn as the morning sun shined its warmth against the garden flowers that fanned out over the yard like a kaleidoscope of color.

"Good morning to you, daughter!" Giovanna's mother was rounding the stone wall on her way to the gate. "And to you Pietro, my new son. Look at these figs. I picked them this morning especially for you." She nodded at a large basket she held in her hand. "It's a beautiful morning, isn't it?"

"Yes!" Giovanna declared with a joy she hadn't felt in years, "It's a beautiful beginning to the day!"

CHAPTER 14

Little Giovanna ran her fingers through the dirt at the base of the zinnias that were just pushing through the earth's surface. The harbor breeze blew over the seedlings creating a flutter of soft green pastels against the black soil. Giovanna didn't notice the creak of the gate or the shiny gold shoes walking into the yard from the other side of the stone wall. It was her grandmother's voice that woke her from her playful fantasy of princesses and warriors within the freshly planted garden.

"Oh Gia!" Nonna Angelina cried with delight, "Look at your white dress. Does your mama know you are in the garden?"

As the words escaped her mouth, Nonna Angelina heard the child's mother respond from the front door.

"No, I didn't. Come here, love." She walked from the house entrance and scooped little Gia up into her arms then turned and kissed her mother on the cheek.

"I remember doing the exact same thing around Nonna's zinnias, " Patrice said. "The flowers were the soldiers and the garden wall, my castle." She smiled.

"Nonna Giovanna would be so pleased to see how Rocco's wife has revived her garden," Angelina said as she held out her hands to meet her granddaughter's and took Giovanna from Patrice.

"It's so funny how Gia went right to that corner of the garden when we arrived." Patrice laughed. "She was miserable on the ferry, cried the whole time but when we walked into the yard, she wanted to get down and then just plopped her butt right there on top of the seedlings and began chattering away."

"Well, it's such a long trip, isn't it? I can understand her misery. Not an easy one for a two-year-old."

Patrice nodded. "She's doing a lot better than her papa! He's still asleep!"

Angelina teased her daughter. "Who told you to marry a weak American?" She laughed. "How's Josh's mother doing? Is she still asleep also?"

Patrice and her family had arrived the night before. She and Josh took up residence in her old bedroom in her parent's house while Josh's mother slept with Gia in Rocco's old bedroom. Josh's mother who had objected to the marriage, had suddenly been transformed on the day of Little Giovanna's birth. It was a transformation that Nonna Angelina completely understood and one for which Patrice was ever so grateful.

Patrice rolled her eyes. "No, she took a walk to the harbor, but she was up all night—with Gia. She insisted. I don't know how either of them are going to make it through the wedding."

"Oh, my little petunia." Angelina looked at Giovanna. "Were you up all night?" She kissed the top of her granddaughter's head.

Little Giovanna yawned as if on cue and the Sunday church bells began to ring as she put her head into the crook of Angelina's neck.

The church bells. Those were Rocco's church bells—their triumphant clang-clang calling to the villagers reminding them of his victorious return. He'd come back from America a rich man after such a short stay, propagating the gold-coins-in-the-American-streets myth. None knew of his whispered conversations with Big Antonio and Maria. The garden was dug up late at night when most were asleep and the few who weren't, attributed the goings on in Pastore di Capre's yard as his ghost coming home to rest, so naturally Rocco and Little Antonio were left undisturbed as they dug up the gold. It didn't take long to find a buyer on the mainland, another advantage of having been locked up for those years before. There were people Rocco knew.

So the church bells, the cement pier, the courtyard garden at the medical center were all recipients of Rocco's new wealth which he deftly distributed so as to erase the gossip of his black luck and replace it with his new returning-as-a-rich-American status. And today was his wedding day!

Now Rocco lay upon his grandparent's sofa. He hadn't the heart to change anything though he could well afford it. He could feel their presence and approval.

His parents had refused to speak to him after his return. They followed days later with the caskets. The services and burial were somber but it was at the burial site that Rocco first laid eyes on the famed Carlo, the foreigner. The gravestone attracted him only because he had so recently hear of Carlo but he hadn't known Carlo's surname. And there it was engraved in stone, making him a real person, someone who had actually existed—Carlo Intruso. Rocco had never believed in the black luck but suddenly he needed to be sure he wasn't stealing from this dead man's family. He elicited Chair's grandson, to help him search the internet for such a name but they just kept hitting dead ends. Finally Chair explained to them that no one knew Carlo's full name, not even Rocco's grandfather. It had been Pastored di Capre's idea to use the man's village of Intruso for the gravestone, but even that was not accurate. Unbeknownst to the villagers, Pastore di Capre had provided it from his imagination. Rocco trusted Chair's grandson now that they were business partners and the tavern has been turned into a pizzeria and by extension he trusted Chair who told them to leave it alone. Let the past stay in the past. And so it did.

Rocco clasped his hands over his chest and adjusted his head on the sofa cushion. He remembered the trip back to Incompresso.

The last leg of it on the ferry, standing at the railing watching the tiny rock in the water emerge and grow to its full island size. As it grew closer his chest heaved with emotion. Small grey specks became houses. He could make out Maria and Big Antonio's house sitting atop his grandparents' house. The harbor came into focus and there was movement—small ant-like crawling movements that slowly became people walking on shore and boats bobbing near the dock. He was overcome by a joy he hadn't expected, a joy of being *home* when home was so elusive for so long.

Angelina and Patrice walked into the small living area.

"Where is the blushing bride?" Angelina asked her son.

But Patrice answered. "Oh, Maria took her up to her house. I was just about to go up there. She's unrelenting, that one. Nonna's friend." Patrice shook her head. "Can't see the groom on the wedding day—bad luck and all that. Rocco's wife didn't want to go with her but well, you know Maria."

Everyone called her *Rocco's wife*, though it was only now, four years after the American woman had shown up to live with Rocco in his grandparent's house that she'd be given the official title bestowed upon her with a wedding ceremony many had anticipated since she'd arrived.

Angelina laughed. "Luck." She shook her head lightly remembering the village whispers about the boy's *black luck*. Certainly there had been none since they'd returned five years before, to bury her parents.

Rocco released a quiet sigh of satisfaction as he put his hands behind his head and looked around the small living area, looked at his mother, his sister, his niece. It was the sigh of a happy man on his wedding day.

"Where's Papa?" he asked Patrice.

"At the tavern seeing to some last minute arrangements for the celebration." Almost everyone, including Patrice still called the new pizzeria the tavern.

At that moment Pasquale was sitting with Chair's grandson at the bar inside the pizzeria. Chair walked toward them with a small pot of espresso. He poured it into the three cups that were already sitting on the bar top and he sat beside the two younger men. They were going over the guest list, which was pretty much the entire island, for who could be excluded without tempting *malocchio*, the evil eye. And God knows Pasquale wasn't going to take any chances with that. Chair agreed, remembering Pastore di Capre's bloody hands the day he came looking for help with Carlo's torn body. He encouraged Angelina and Pasquale to put out a general invitation to all as insurance for their son's future.

The tables were set in long rows at the front of the tavern under the portico roof. Each was draped with a rose-colored tablecloth. At the insistence of the American bride, three crystal vases were placed at the center of the long tables readied for the bouquets of local wild roses that Chair's grandson had stored in the walk-in refrigerator of the newly refinished pizzeria kitchen. If need be, they would spill more tables out onto the road, depending on who showed up, for it was not the usual custom to respond to an invitation other than a mention of it from an invitee on the street or in the market or at church. So the preparation was for the entire village and the expectation was that all would come, which is actually what happened later that day.

In the meantime, Rocco's bride sat at the table in Maria's kitchen as Anna Maria applied the last minute touches to her hair. Rocco, his tailored suit hanging in the closet of the bedroom that he and his bride had shared for the last four years, continued to sit on the sofa as his sister went into the kitchen to find a wet towel for Little Gia's muddy hands.

And Rocco continued to revel in his fantasy of how life would proceed — finally marrying the woman he loved. They'd communicated via telephone after Chair's grandson showed him the nuances of Facetime and texting. It was a relationship that blossomed through satellite connections. And when she'd finally arrived, he was overcome with a joy that translated to a man ready for a wife and family. They only needed to wait for the necessary paperwork, which sometimes took eons with the Italian bureaucracy and the American red tape. No one had expected it to be so long—four years. But Rocco didn't care, nor did his American bride for they were together—though Rocco insisted everything be in order, everything legal, so a wedding was planned and re-planned until finally all the papers were in order.

A commotion at the side of the house woke Rocco from his reverie.

"No, no," it was Maria's voice, "you cannot see the groom. It's bad luck. Not today!"

With a flourish of white, his beautiful bride, pushed through the door. Maria, and Angelina followed. Baby Giovanna, in Angelina's arms grabbed at the bride's veil and left a smudge of brown in the tulle. Maria gasped. Rocco laughed.

"It's okay. Relax everyone," he said as he rose from the sofa.

There she was, his beautiful American bride: Javier's daughter, Rosa.

CHAPTER 15

"Here, use my sunglasses," he said.

"No, I can see perfectly," she answered him with a quick glance and a smile.

"The sun isn't too strong?" he asked.

"Not at all. I like it. "

"It *is* beautiful here. The light is so striking. It's all so clear."

"Hm." It was an answer of agreement.

He watched her drive, her hands firmly on the steering wheel, the winding road hugging the mountain as she followed its sharp turns perched along the edges of its rocky girth. Small houses clung together below in the valley like unconnected beads that have fallen haphazardly from a string.

"Oh, look at that hamlet down there." She'd seen it too. "It's adorable, isn't it?"

"Keep your eyes on the road," Joe chuckled, "precious cargo aboard."

He turned slightly to see four-year-old Regina watching from her car seat. The images from the car window were like moving ribbons of color.

Gina reached over and rubbed Joe's arm.

"I know," she said, "I know."

One more curve and then a sudden stretch of white sea lay

atop the distant hills as the car descended from the mountains.

They both gasped from the surprise of it.

"Oh." It was said in a whispered unison.

The move from Robin's Nest had been an easy one, a move they'd agreed was long overdue. Now as the road wound its way along the edges of the hills and the sea opened into a sparkle of light, they knew this was the correct place for them.

California.

"What Mommy? Daddy?" asked little Regina. "What do you see?"

"Our future," Joe said and he gave his wife a little wink.

ABOUT THE AUTHOR

Linda Fagioli-Katsiotas lives on Long Island with her husband, Nick. She teaches English to newly immigrated English language learners at her local public school. She is also a speech pathologist working with adults who have brain injury. Although *Among the Zinnias* was inspired by these two roles, it remains a work of fiction.

Independent authors often have quite a challenge in getting exposure for their work. I hope, dear reader, you will consider writing a review on Amazon or Goodreads.com.

You can visit Linda Fagioli-Katsiotas' blog The Nifi at: www.truestorythenifi.blogspot.com

Linda Fagioli-Katsiotas

A SPECIAL THANKS

To Doreen Ciabattari-Malloy for her overwhelming enthusiasm
and for her editorial suggestions.

YOUR OWN KIND

Your Own Kind is based on much of the author's experience as a waitress in the 1970s and 1980s. Though it is fiction, it touches upon many situations that were common place in those days in the seaside village where she lived.

It is 1974. Alexandros is a young man who has left his rural Greek village to come to New York to work in his cousin's restaurant. The restaurant is in East End, a small hamlet fifty miles from New York City—not exactly what Alexandros had expected when he heard he'd be going to New York.

Sarah is from a small town in the mountains of New York State. She has moved to East End to escape the sins of her past. Of course, she and Alexandros fall in love—no surprise to the readers. But their different cultures and traditions stand in their way, as Alexandros is betrothed to a girl back home and Sarah has a secret that would deter Alexandros regardless of the situation. Add to that, one love-sick adolescent, whose jealousy, thirst for revenge and misinterpretation of events set in motion a series of actions that lead to violence and heartbreak. Maybe life would be easier if people would just stick with their own kind. But what does that actually mean?

Michele James of Book Chat wrote: *Your Own Kind explores the ins and outs of relationships where all is not as it seems. I would recommend Your Own Kind to anyone who enjoys fiction with well defined characters and a believable story.*

Linda Fagioli-Katsiotas

A MEMOIR

In Greek, the word "nifi" is used to describe a woman who marries into a family. *The Nifi* is, in part, the story of the author's journey in which she struggles to keep her identity in a culture that threatens to swallow her whole. It is also juxtaposed with that of her mother-in-law, Chevi, who gladly welcomes her into the family, though they speak no common language.

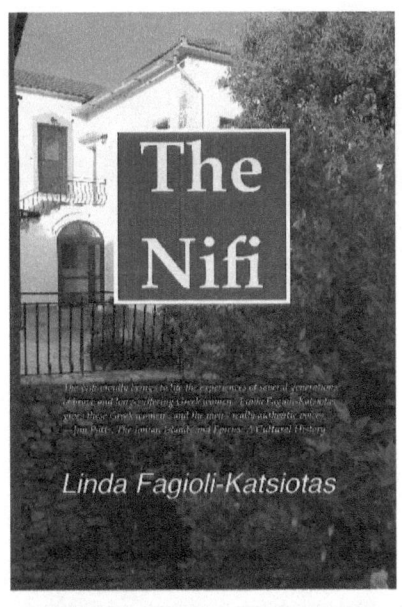

Chevi, through the translation of her son, and then years later as the author begins to learn Greek, conveys her story, a life which is rife with heartache and betrayal. She is no less than a heroine who quietly fights against the patriarchal society that dictates her every movement. Those stories which Chevi repeated often as though she feared they'd be lost forever, ultimately inspired the memoir, *The Nifi*.

The Nifi opens in 1983 in the village of Margariti in Epirus, Greece. In addition to a new unknown language, the author is faced with a lack of running water, poor roadways, no way to contact her family back in the U.S. and a mind-numbing culture shock. A month before, in a New York suburb she'd married her husband in an impulsive moment of passion after having worked with him at a local restaurant for a short period of time. With her inexperience and with mounds of unrealistic romanticism, she'd agreed to travel to his village and stay for an undefined period of time.

British author, Jim Potts, in his review of The Nifi writes: *The Nifi vividly brings to life the experiences of several generations of brave and long-suffering Greek women, as well as gives these Greek women—and men—authentic voices. . . It's a very honest and utterly convincing true story. It's a pity that there are not more accounts written by Epirote women. . .*

Linda Fagioli-Katsiotas